Praise for the AM

D1140009

'A great tale, which builds in intensity as the story unfolds.
For children who have not been introduced to fantasy, this
would definitely be a great book to begin with' *School Librarian*

'A charming, inventive children's fantasy, which reminds me
of early Diana Wynne Jones'
Katherine Langrish, author of *Troll Fell*

'*Deep Amber* has pace, humour and inventiveness . . .
There's a crackle of magic in the atmosphere and a rapidly
thickening plot' Julia Jones, author of *The Salt-Stained Book*

'Delightful . . . A cross between the early Harry Potter books
and *The Magician's Nephew* by C. S. Lewis'
Catherine on *Goodreads*

'Fantasy, with lots of humour . . . and a very exciting finale,'
Emma Barnes, author of *Wolfie* and *Wild Thing*

'Exciting and hilarious' Catherine Butler,

000000953209

Books by C. J. Busby

The *Amber* series
Deep Amber
Dragon Amber
The Amber Crown

The *Spell* series
Frogspell
Cauldron Spells
Icespell
Swordspell

THE
AMBER
CROWN

C. J. Busby

templar

First published in Great Britain in 2015
by Templar Publishing
Northburgh House, 10 Northburgh Street,
London EC1V 0AT
www.templarco.co.uk

Text copyright © C. J. Busby, 2015
Illustrations copyright © David Wyatt, 2015

The moral rights of the author and illustrator have been asserted.

All rights reserved. No part of this publication may be
reproduced, stored or transmitted in any form by any means,
electronic, mechanical, photocopying or otherwise, without the
prior written permission of the publisher.

A CIP catalogue record for this book is available
from the British Library.

ISBN: 978–1–783–70198–8
3 5 7 9 10 8 6 4 2
Printed and bound by Clays Ltd, St Ives plc

Templar Publishing is part of the Bonnier Publishing Group
www.bonnierpublishing.com

For Laura

DUDLEY PUBLIC LIBRARIES	
000000953209	
£6.99	JF
23-Apr-2015	PETERS
JFP	

Prologue

Lord Ravenglass stood by the arched window of his chamber, looking out over the roofs of the city. The pale towers of the palace gleamed in the sunset, but dusk was gently settling on the rest of the city below. He watched the shadows deepen, thinking about the piece of deep amber he'd so nearly had in his grasp. He could see it in his mind's eye – the glowing, orange-brown teardrop with its ornate clasp of bronze leaves.

Maybe he should just have killed the girl, he thought, absently fingering his lace cuffs. Once she'd given him the earth amber, he could have blasted her and her brother to little heaps of dust on the floor of the palace cellars. Then they wouldn't have had a chance to steal it back and disappear.

He sighed. He would have done it, left to himself. He would happily have reduced the two meddling children to nothingness. But Lukos had turned out to be right, as usual. Letting them live, even letting them escape, was going to reap a much larger reward than killing them.

Ravenglass thought about the first time he'd met Lukos. He'd been a mere boy, exploring the palace cellars. Deep in a forgotten corner he'd found an invisible barrier and a man imprisoned behind it in silver chains. Locked up, his very name erased from memory, for being too adventurous, too ambitious. *I can see you're the same, boy*, he'd said. *We're alike, you and me. You've got power and the will to use it. You're not like most of the useless milk-sops who find me.*

Lord Ravenglass stroked his chin and smiled, remembering. He'd felt special, Lukos's favourite; the boy who wasn't afraid to question, to experiment. And Lukos had taught him so much. The dark magic of the crow karls. The truth about the forest and the Great Tree and the so-called worlds of light. The way the forest folk had tricked and stolen the worlds from the creatures of darkness. Ravenglass knew now that

Lukos was the half-brother of the ancient king, Bruni. The king had betrayed Lukos, imprisoned him in a world of ice and snow, and destroyed his followers. Now Ravenglass would be the one to release him, overthrow the forest and destroy all the current worlds of light. Then he would rule over a new realm, with Lukos to advise him and guide him. And to teach him the magic of immortality…

There was a noise near the door and Ravenglass turned, his eyebrows raised. Two tall, thin men in black suits stood at the entrance to the chambers.

"My lord," said the first, in a dry, rasping voice.

"Mr Jones," said Lord Ravenglass coldly. "Mr Smith."

"We have located the ship that carries the sea amber, and we are making ready to set sail. Preparations will be completed tomorrow."

"Good," said Lord Ravenglass. "This almost makes up for your incompetence in Ur-Akkad. And a portal key for Wemworthy?"

Mr Jones held out a small chip of dark metal. "From a lamp-post," he said. "At the end of the road."

Lord Ravenglass took the metal and slipped

it into his pocket, waving Smith and Jones away with his other hand. He turned back to the window, peering at the fading light. The spell Lukos had told him to put on the boy Simon would be starting to work just about now. It would be creeping into Simon's mind, rearranging his thoughts, persuading him that the man Simon had seen trapped in the ice cave was not Lukos, Lord of Wolves, but Gwyn Arnold, his own father. Making him think that the best way to help his father was to return to the kingdom, to Lord Ravenglass, and that above all he had to bring the pieces of deep amber – the earth amber his sister Catrin possessed, and the fire amber that the forest agents had snatched before Smith and Jones could get to it.

Lord Ravenglass rested his forehead against the cool glass of the window and smiled. *Soon*, he thought. *Soon*.

Chapter One

Simon woke in darkness, the after-images of fragmented dreams starting to fade from his mind. He tried to reach for them, but they were disappearing into shadow. Only two images remained: the thin figure of his father – blue eyes burning in his pale face, the ice and snow of his solitary prison stretching out all around – and the dark, curly ringlets of Lord Ravenglass falling forward as he bent towards Simon, rings sparkling on the elegant fingers of his outstretched hand.

Lord Ravenglass. And Dad. Except… *Was* it his dad? Simon started to wake up properly. He felt hot, feverish, and his head was pounding. Hadn't he been told the man in the ice cave *wasn't* Gwyn Arnold – *wasn't* the father he'd thought was dead? Simon strained after the memory, but it was just a wisp. All that remained was a sense that he'd been lied to, that *someone* had tried to prevent him from helping his dad escape that prison, and that he had to do something, now, before it was too late.

Simon sat up. The house was silent. He tried to gather his thoughts, but they were like cobwebs, breaking every time he tried to grasp them. He was at home, he knew that. He could just make out a hunched-up figure lying on his floor, entirely wrapped in a duvet, like a large, cocooned slug. Jem. It was Jem – the castle kitchen boy from the kingdom. Simon rubbed his face, trying to remember. Jem had been here yesterday with the apprentice witch Dora. And there had been someone else with them… a girl with deep brown skin and jewelled braids. Inanna! That was it. Princess Inanna, from the Akkadian Empire.

Suddenly Simon's mind cleared. He knew exactly what he needed to do. Inanna had a piece of deep amber – she'd brought it with her from Ur-Akkad. She had the fire amber, and his sister, Cat, had the earth amber, the very first piece of deep amber they'd found – the one that had opened the rift to the kingdom and brought Lord

Ravenglass and his henchmen to their world. If Simon was going to save his dad, he needed both pieces of deep amber. He had to take them back to the kingdom and hand them over to Lord Ravenglass.

Simon eased himself off the bed and started to pull on his clothes. Jem stirred slightly under his duvet, and Simon paused, holding his breath. It wasn't long before Jem's breathing became regular again, and Simon reached out for his hoody. As he pulled it on, there was a faint chirruping sound. Frizzle! Simon put his hand in the pocket and felt the warm, furry body of the little creature. He was a bit like a hamster, if you didn't peer too closely – a hamster with fluffy grey feathers and two stubby wings. But he'd flown into Simon's bedroom through a portal from another world. As Simon stroked Frizzle's ears, he felt a momentary confusion. What was he doing? Should he be sneaking out like this? Maybe he'd better wake Cat and talk to her about it.

But then a stabbing pain lanced through his head and he almost doubled over, holding his knees and gasping. As it passed, so did his momentary doubt. He couldn't wake Cat. She wouldn't let him leave. She had been tricked by the forest agent Albert Jemmet, and by Uncle Lou – she didn't believe the man in the ice was truly their dad.

Calmer now, Simon reached out for his sword. It was lying at the foot of his bed, the faint light from the window picking out the engraved patterns on the blade. It had belonged to his father, but long before that it had been forged by the one-eyed king, Bruni, out of metal from every world. Simon pushed it into the makeshift strap he'd secured to his belt, then crept across the room and let himself out.

Cat's bedroom door was ajar, and in the faint moonlight from her window he could see three sleeping figures. Inanna's dark braids were spread out on the pillow of Cat's bed, and Cat and Dora were huddled under blankets on the floor. Simon stood in the doorway, his eyes gradually adjusting to the light, and then he stepped softly inside the room.

On the dressing table next to the bed was a faintly glowing pool of light. Inanna's amber pendant sat on a golden chain, flickering with a bright, fiery orange light. Sitting next to it, in the

14

middle of the dressing table, was an open wooden box. It had three strange symbols carved into the lid, and it, too, glowed slightly. Simon scooped the pendant into the box, and then looked down at Cat. She was huddled up sideways, her head resting in the crook of one arm, the other flung out across the blanket. Her short blonde hair was sticking up, and around her neck Simon could see a bronze chain, intertwined with a silver one. Delicately, he unclasped the bronze chain, and drew it out from under her sleeping body. As the last few links unwound themselves from the silver chain, Cat opened her eyes and Simon froze.

"Simon?" she said fuzzily, barely focusing.

"It's all right," he murmured. "Go back to sleep."

"Mmm – s'not morning yet?" she said, her eyelids fluttering.

"No – not morning. It's nothing. Go to sleep."

She subsided, tucking her arm back under the blanket. Simon, who'd been holding his breath, let it out slowly, and held up the pendant he'd taken from her. The dark amber teardrop gleamed, whorls of orange and brown glinting and moving in its depths. He dropped it into the wooden box with the other pendant and shut the lid firmly.

Simon slipped out of the bedroom and down the stairs. The door to the living room was half open. He paused, looking in. Uncle Lou was sprawled on the sofa, one arm flung out across the maps and almanacs scattered on the nearby coffee table. His face was pale, his black hair damp with sweat and his breathing shallow. His wrist was bandaged and a faint stain of blood was visible on his shirt from the wound Smith and Jones had given him. On the floor nearby, Sir Bedwyr was on his back, snoring loudly.

Simon watched Lou for a moment. He had been Dad's best friend, one of the agents of the Great Forest. In the kingdom, he was known as the Druid. He'd helped bring Cat and Simon for a while in this world after Dad had died… Simon blinked. *No*, not after he'd died. After he'd been *betrayed* and chained in that ice cave. By the forest agents. By the Druid.

Simon's grip tightened on the box with the ambers, and he tiptoed along the hallway, easing open the front door and then closing it again with just the faintest click. Outside, it was still dark. The night air was cool and sharp. Simon inhaled and felt suddenly giddy. Half of him was triumphant, excited, glad that he'd soon be at the palace and one step nearer to rescuing his dad. The other half felt strangely subdued, and there was a small knot of tension in his stomach that he couldn't explain. *Nerves*, he thought. *Just nerves*.

He set off down the street to where a shadowy figure was waiting. A tall man with dark ringlets and an elegant ruffled coat, standing in the pool of yellow light cast by a nearby street lamp.

Chapter Two

Princess Inanna was the first to realise that something was wrong. Waking in a strange bed, in peculiar clothes, she'd taken a moment to remember that she was no longer in Ur-Akkad, first city of the Akkadian Empire. She was no longer a priestess in the Temple of Ishtar. She was in another world, one with a kind of magic they called 'electricity'. She had escaped, with Dora and Jem, as the civilisation she'd known all her life collapsed around her, its technology no longer powered by the piece of amber they'd taken with them when they fled. The fire amber.

Inanna sat up and reached out for the amber necklace, but it wasn't where she'd left it the night before. She frowned, and hung her head over the edge of the bed, feeling around on the floor to see if it had slipped off the cupboard.

"Cat!" she said, poking the lump of blankets next to the bed. "Cat! Where's my amber? Did you put it somewhere?"

"Mmmph…" came a muffled response from under the covers. "Nanna. Go b' sleep. S'twirly."

"What?' said Inanna. "Cat! Dora! Wake up!" She shoved the sleeping figure next to her with one hand, and then reached out a foot to nudge the other pile of blankets. "One of you's asleep on my amber. I want it – now!"

Dora's pale face and neat dark plaits emerged from the other side of Cat and she blinked owlishly at Inanna.

"Your amber?" said Dora. "Isn't it round your neck?"

"No," said Inanna impatiently. "I took it off. I didn't want to strangle myself in the night. It was here – on this cupboard. But it's fallen off. Or – " her eyes grew round – "it's been stolen!"

Dora suddenly felt very wide awake. Stolen? But did that mean…? Could Smith and Jones have worked out where they'd gone? Could they have followed them to the house – broken the wards they'd set the night before? She shook Cat's shoulder.

"Cat! Wake up! Inanna thinks her amber's gone. Have you got yours?"

For a moment Cat didn't respond and Dora wasn't sure she'd heard. But then she sat up in a rush, her hand clutching at her throat. Dora could see that the pendant, with its deep orange-brown stone, was no longer round her neck. Only her silver locket remained, gleaming in the faint morning light.

Dora pulled back the blankets from where they had spilled over the floor, and lifted the edge of the mattress. She felt under the bed and then under the cupboard, while Inanna and Cat watched her, the two of them seemingly stunned. After a few moments, she looked up and shook her head.

"They've gone. Both pieces."

Cat's mum Florence was in the kitchen, cooking up a large pan of scrambled eggs while Albert Jemmet buttered endless rounds of toast. The portly forest agent glanced up as Dora ran into the room.

"Morning, Dora! Ready for some breakfast?"

"The pieces of amber – they've gone!" cried

Dora, as Cat and Inanna tumbled into the room behind her. "Inanna left hers on the bedside cupboard – but Cat's was round her neck. And they've both disappeared!"

Albert frowned, putting down the knife he was holding. He wiped his hands deliberately on his blue overalls and then extracted a small box from one of his many pockets. Twiddling a few knobs, he scanned the dials on the box quickly and then looked up.

"No one's broken the wards," he said. "But neither of the amber jewels are here. Readings are way down."

He glanced across at Florence. "You'd better wake Lou. And you –" he pointed at Dora and the others – "go and get Jem and Simon. Something's not right here."

"I'll get them," said Cat, her face white. She set off up the stairs, taking them two at a time, as Florence headed for the living room. Inanna sat down at the kitchen table and burst into tears.

"It was *my* amber!" she wailed. "I'd only just got it! I'd managed to do magic with it. And now it's *gone!*" She put her head on her arms and sobbed.

Dora patted her on the back sympathetically,

but she felt more like shaking her. If the amber had gone, there was more to worry about than Inanna not being able to do magic with it. If it was in the hands of Lord Ravenglass, then he was a whole lot closer to remaking the amber crown. And if he managed that, then they'd have to deal with Lukos, the Lord of Wolves, and all the powers of the dark from before the worlds were made. Dora felt sick. She'd faced the dark-suited crow men, Smith and Jones, and she'd do it again if she had to. But everything she'd heard about Lukos made her want to turn herself into a tiny mouse and hide in a hole somewhere far away.

There was a clattering on the stairs, and Cat came running into the kitchen. Jem was behind her, his red hair falling over his freckled face, his expression bewildered.

"Simon's not here!" said Cat. "He's gone! He must have been kidnapped. And *he* –" she turned to Jem and thumped him rather hard on the shoulder – "he was fast asleep! Didn't hear a thing!"

"Ow!" Jem rubbed his shoulder and looked at Cat resentfully. "I can't help it if I didn't wake up. They must have put a spell on me or something. Normally I'm a very light sleeper."

Dora, worried as she was, couldn't help snorting with laughter. Jem wouldn't wake up if an earthquake happened right underneath him. In fact, she wasn't sure he was totally awake even now. Something in his blurry expression made her suspect he was only using half his brain while he waited for the other half to wake up.

Inanna raised her head and wiped her tears with the back of her hand, sniffing loudly. "Jem!" she said mournfully. "My amber's gone. It's gone! And after I mastered it, too!"

Cat made an exasperated noise. "Yes – well mine's gone too, in case you hadn't noticed. And so has my *brother*! Disappeared! And we don't know where he is, or who might have taken him!"

Her voice was gradually getting higher and more hysterical, and she looked as if she might just punch Inanna on her royal nose.

"All right, all right, calm down," said Albert sternly. "Jem, go and look in the garden and round the house, see if you can find anything. Dora, go with him, he looks half asleep. Cat, check in every room upstairs. And, Inanna –" he pointed to the large teapot on the kitchen table and handed her some mugs – "pour us all a nice mug of tea.

Twelve sugars for me. It helps me think."

Dora steered Jem to the back door and they slipped into the garden, just as Florence and the Druid came into the kitchen. Dora could hear the Druid's urgent questions and Albert's calm voice explaining what had happened. Quietly she closed the door behind them and took a careful look around.

It was early – the sky was pale, the trees like inky shadows at the edges of the garden. There was dew on the grass, and a fresh, cool smell. Gradually Dora let her senses expand outwards, across the garden, around the house. Finally she relaxed. There wasn't the slightest hint of magic nearby. There were no black crow feathers on the grass. She couldn't feel even the edge of a shadow of Smith and Jones's presence.

Jem strode across the lawn and peered at the trees, looking up into the branches as if he half expected Simon to be perched there amongst the leaves. Then he examined the back wall intently.

"Umm… what are you doing?" said Dora.

Jem turned to her with a glazed expression in his green eyes. "Looking. For Simon. Or clues. Or whatever we're supposed to be doing."

"Jem!" said Dora, and snapped her fingers in front of his face. "Concentrate!" She directed a very small awakening spell at him and the glazed expression lifted from his face like early morning mist.

"Dora!" he said. "Did someone say both pieces of amber were gone? *And* Simon?"

Chapter Three

The cellars of the palace were cool and dimly lit. Lord Ravenglass strode ahead, the box containing the two amber jewels held firmly under his arm. Simon followed, hands in his pockets, stroking Frizzle's ruffled feathers. He couldn't shake off a sense that he was doing something terribly wrong and betraying everyone back home in Wemworthy. But they wouldn't understand, he told himself fiercely. He had to help rescue Dad, whatever it took. Cat and Mum had been tricked. They thought the forest agents were on their side, but they weren't. It was the forest agents that had betrayed Dad in the first place. Only Ravenglass had stayed true. Only Ravenglass had stuck by Dad.

Simon found himself going over these thoughts

again and again, round and round in circles. But however many times he repeated them, they still somehow felt wrong.

He and Ravenglass were at the spiral staircase now, and a blueish white light was seeping up the stairwell, illuminating the way down. Simon could almost feel the cold of his dad's icy prison. Ravenglass turned and smiled at him, his white teeth gleaming in his handsome face.

"Ready, Simon? Your father will be *so* pleased to see you again!"

Simon nodded, and found his hand on the hilt of his sword. He remembered the sword training he'd done with Lord Ravenglass just yesterday down in these same cellars – thrust and parry and thrust, with Dad looking on, encouraging and proud, from the cave where he'd been trapped all those years ago. Simon straightened his shoulders and made his way down the stairs.

"We have the amber!" announced Lord Ravenglass as he approached the invisible barrier that divided the cellar from Gwyn's world. "Simon has brought us both pieces." His voice was dripping with satisfaction, the box held out with a flourish.

Standing at the barrier was a gaunt figure with startling blue eyes. His clothes were worn thin, his skin blemished with sores where he was manacled to silver chains that stretched out behind him to a dark cave. A mountain of ice loomed above the cave, and all around was a vast expanse of ice and snow. Yet despite his ragged clothes, the man was not shivering. There was a sense of power in his movements, the strength and grace of an animal. His gaze flicked from the box to Simon.

"You came back then," he said, his voice hoarse, rasping, as if it was rarely used.

"I brought the amber," said Simon. "Both pieces. They're in the box."

"Open it," commanded the man, his expression intent, almost feverish.

Lord Ravenglass placed the box on the floor. Then he gestured at it with a flick of his fingers and said the words of the opening spell. The strange triangular symbols on the box glowed, and immediately a sheet of bright flames rose up around it. They were extinguished rapidly as the box became covered in a layer of frost, and then finally a small hurricane appeared out of nowhere, blowing Simon's hair back from his face as the box opened. Inside were the two amber stones, the dark orange-brown teardrop with its bronze clasp of leaves, and the dazzling yellow-orange fire amber, its gold chain and ornate clasp gleaming in the reflected light of the two jewels.

The man behind the barrier breathed in deeply and closed his eyes. After a few moments, he opened them and smiled – and Simon felt his stomach clench. It was not a nice smile. It was hungry, crooked, and it made him look like a different person. Then, like a passing shadow, the expression was gone, and the man was his father again. He grinned at Simon and pressed his hand up against the wall of solid air that separated them.

"Well done, Simon," he said. "Well done. We're nearly there!"

Simon reached out and pressed his hand opposite his father's, but the barrier held them firmly apart. It was only a few centimetres, but it might as well have been a thousand miles. Simon longed to be able to push his way through, to feel his dad's arms around him, to feel warm and safe and glad that he had done the right thing.

Instead, he just felt hollow, and the tight knot of tension in his stomach stubbornly refused to dissolve.

Lord Ravenglass came up behind him and rested his hand on Simon's shoulder. "Yes, well done, young man. Two bits of amber. *And* the sword!"

"The sword?" said Simon, putting his hand on the hilt. "Do you need that too?"

Gwyn nodded, his gaze intent. "The sword will be exceedingly useful – but so will you, Simon. We need you to wield it."

Simon frowned. "But Lord Ravenglass is a better swordsman. Why me?"

"You are descended in an unbroken line from Bruni's youngest son. That's to say –" Gwyn laughed, and exchanged glances with Lord Ravenglass – "*I* am descended from Bruni's son. So of course, you are, too. Unfortunately, Ravenglass here, dear as he is to me, is related to Bruni through his mother – the queen's sister. He can't wield the full power of the sword."

Simon felt his uncertainty dissolve in a burst of pride. The sword was special, he'd always felt that – and now it was clear that it was *meant* to be his, it had always been meant for him. No one else could use its full power.

"Of course," he said. "I'll do whatever needs doing."

"Good," said Gwyn. "I knew I could rely on you." He glanced across at Ravenglass, and gave him the slightest nod. "We will need you at the making. But first – we need you to help us get the sky amber."

"How?" said Simon. "What do I have to do?"

"We need to get the amber from the queen," said Lord Ravenglass, his mouth twisting with dislike. "And we need to do it soon, in case the forest agents get to her, warn her we have you and the other pieces of amber. Queen Igraine might be a bit old and deaf but she's not an idiot. And she's a formidable magic user. Much stronger than I am. Even with two pieces of amber, I can't stand against her. But the sword – Bruni's sword, wielded by a direct heir – can be used to defend us against her magic."

Gwyn leaned forward against the barrier, his eyes boring into Simon's, his expression intent. "With the sword to protect him, Ravenglass will be immune to her spells. He can force her to give

31

up the amber to him. So we need you, Simon. We need you to learn how to use the sword to stop magic. Can you do that?"

Simon met his dad's gaze. "I'll do my best," he said.

Gwyn relaxed, and smiled, and Simon smiled back. He was going to do it. He was going to save his dad. Mum and Cat were going to be so amazed when they found out he'd been right all along. Gwyn would be free, and they would all be together again. A proper family.

Chapter Four

Dora and Jem slipped back into the kitchen just as Sir Bedwyr stumbled in from the living room, his black hair sticking out in all directions. He was followed by the ghostly figure of Great-Aunt Irene. The others were all seated at the kitchen table and Cat had her head in her hands.

"He came in," she was saying, as Dora took the empty chair next to her. "I thought it was a dream – I must have been half asleep. But I can remember Simon bending over me and… I think he must have been pulling the chain off my neck." She raised her head, her expression bewildered. "He must have taken it. He must have taken both of them. But *why*…?"

Albert Jemmet was tapping his teeth thoughtfully with a wooden toothpick. "Spell," he said heavily. "We should have guessed. Ravenglass must have realised he'd broken the previous enchantment and put another one on him – one that activated last night. He'll have gone to the kingdom. Taken both pieces with him."

"Unless…" said Florence in a small voice. "Unless he really believed it all along. That it *is* his dad in there. In that ice cave."

Albert shook his head. "No. I talked to him, when I found him in the palace. He'd nearly shaken off that spell of Ravenglass's already. When I got to him it was just rags and tatters."

A tear ran down Florence's face. "I should have told them about their dad all along. About the magic and the kingdom. I should have been honest with them. Maybe all this would never have happened."

Cat got up to give her mum a hug, and they clung to each other for a while. "It's my fault, too," said Cat. "If I'd woken up properly I could have stopped him."

Sir Bedwyr, who'd appeared a little confused up till then, gave Cat a deep bow and put his hand firmly on his sword hilt. "My lady. If there is anything I can do to remedy your distress. Any enemies I can smite. Just say the word."

Cat looked over at the handsome knight, with his earnest face, and found the corner of her mouth twitching. "Thank you, Sir Bedwyr," she said, with an attempt at a curtsey. "But I'm not sure what you can do just now."

"That," said Great-Aunt Irene, rapping her silvery cane on the table, "is precisely what we are here to decide. There's no point worrying about who's to blame. It seems to me it's Ravenglass that's to blame and that's an end of it. What's important now is what we do about it."

"Quite so," said the Druid, and gestured to Sir Bedwyr to sit down. "We need to make plans."

"I'm going to get Simon," said Cat, lifting her chin. "And it's no good looking at me like that, Mum. I've been there – I know the palace. I can sneak in and find him, I'm sure. I have to do something! He's in terrible danger!"

Florence pressed her lips together. "You're not going, Cat," she said. "I'm not risking both of you. If anyone's going to go and get Simon, it's going to be me."

Cat gaped at her mother.

"You?" she said. "But, Mum – you can't! It's…

it's another world. It's got magic and…"

Florence looked at her sternly. "Cat – I was married to your dad for fifteen years. To say nothing of putting up with Lou for most of that time and beyond. I do know a little bit about magic. And as it happens, I know the Royal City quite well. I'm not sitting here at home while Simon's in the kingdom, being lied to by that foul… Thinking his dad…" She stopped, and took a deep breath. "I'm going to get him and bring him home."

The Druid hesitated, and then nodded. "I think I agree," he said. "Florence should go."

"Then I'm going with her!" said Cat. "You can't leave me behind. I *have* to go!"

Druid shook his head. "We need you here, Cat. You and Iannna. We have to get Simon, but we also have to go to the Adamantine Sea. We have to find the sea amber – and for that, we have to have an heir. Someone who can sense it, and control it. You need to be here, learning that control, ready to go as soon as we've located the right place."

"Indeed," said Great-Aunt Irene. "It's no good rescuing Simon if we let Ravenglass get the last piece of amber. If he remakes the crown, then he destroys all the worlds of light. No one will be rescuing anyone if that happens."

"He *what*?" said Cat, shocked. "I thought… Well, I mean, I know he'll release Lukos, but…" Her voice trailed away.

Albert Jemmet looked around the table and sighed. "I'm afraid it's true," he said. "Lukos's prison is made from slivers of all worlds and all times. To break it open, the boundaries of those worlds will have to be dissolved. It will be chaos – the energy flows will cause hurricanes, tidal waves, whole countries slipping between worlds, times getting tangled up. The Tree will almost certainly split into fragments. Most people alive in those worlds will die – a few will find themselves in the only place that remains. A realm ruled by the dark."

There was silence round the table.

"But it's not going to happen," said Albert at last. "Because we're going to stop him. And that –" he pointed his toothpick at Cat – "is why you have to stay here and practise your magic."

"He's right," said the Druid. "But it's also true that Florence can't go on her own. So – I'll go with her."

Albert coughed. "You're in no state to go anywhere, Lou," he said. "Broken wrist. Nasty stab wound to the chest. Not sure you could conjure so much as a sugar bowl right now."

The Druid frowned and waggled the fingers of his left hand where they emerged from the bandages. "The wrist's healing nicely. I've got very strong bones. And I feel fine." He flicked his fingers at the kitchen table. Then he flicked them again. He focused, moved his hand more slowly over the table and muttered the words of a spell. Nothing happened.

Albert picked up his mug and took a noisy slurp of tea. "I rest my case," he said, and the Druid rubbed his chin, and laughed.

"OK," he said. "You're right. I'm not entirely myself. But I know the kingdom and I know Lukos. Florence needs someone with her who's not walking into the situation blind."

"I'll go with her," said Albert. "And while we're at it, we need to get the queen. Ravenglass has two pieces of deep amber now. He's still not a match for the queen, but it's too close to risk it. We have to remove her and the sky amber before he can take it from her."

The Druid nodded, but his brown eyes were anxious as he turned back to Florence. "You'll be careful?" he said. "Ravenglass is very powerful. And Lukos can't do magic through that barrier, but he's still dangerous. He can influence people… in all sorts of ways."

"Don't worry, Lou," said Florence grimly. "I won't let him trick me into thinking he's Gwyn." She looked at him meaningfully. "Or anyone else I care for."

The Druid coloured, and Albert pushed his chair back and stood up.

"Well, no time like the present," he said, patting his pockets and extracting a small metal doorknob. He held it up to show them. "This will take us to the forest's city agent. He's got a nice out-of-the-way attic room in the western quarter. From there we can find out what's happening, scope out the best way into the palace." He turned to the Druid. "But before I go… you might find these useful." He pulled a key out of another of his pockets and threw it into a bowl on the kitchen table. "Key to my lock-up," he said to the Druid. "Lots of useful items there." Then he fished a golden-orange leaf out of another one of his overall pockets and flourished it. "And my pass. Straight to the heart of the forest."

"That takes you to the Great Forest?" said Jem, looking awed. "Does every agent get one?"

Albert twirled it between his fingers. "Indeed they do, young Jem. But not until they've earned it. So I'll be giving this one to the Druid, for safe keeping."

Dora could see from Jem's expression that his long-held ambition to be a knight was struggling with a new desire to be a forest agent. She bit her lip. It seemed such a slim chance that they could still stop Ravenglass – get the sea amber before he or the crow men got there, and get the queen and the sky amber out of the palace. But if they failed, the chances of Jem surviving to be either a knight or a forest agent were pretty low.

Albert held out the metal doorknob and said the words of the portal spell. A swirling area of white mist formed in the middle of the kitchen.

"Florence?" he said, and she stood up.

Cat threw her arms round her mum's neck and hugged her tight. "Good luck," she whispered. "Find Simon. Make sure he's all right."

Florence smiled, and hugged her back.

"Look after Cat," she said sternly to the Druid, and then gestured at the others round the table. "Keep them *all* safe."

She took a last look around the kitchen and then walked into the misty portal with Albert striding firmly after her. Behind them, the mist popped out of existence.

There was a moment's silence in the kitchen. Then the Druid ran his hands through his messy black hair and stood up.

"I promised I'd keep you safe," he said, looking round at them all. "But the best way of doing that is making sure Ravenglass doesn't get the last piece of amber. Cat and Inanna, you have to learn to send your magic out to objects if you're going to be able to find the sea amber. And then you have to get to the Adamantine Sea before Smith and Jones do. It might be our only chance of stopping Ravenglass from remaking the crown."

Chapter Five

The Adamantine Sea moved between worlds with a complex but predictable cycle. According to the Druid's calculations, it was currently touching the port of Belhaven, on the wet and windy isle of Skarron. The world that the isle was found in was an old one, with hardly any modern gadgets and not much magic either.

"It's rather like the sixteenth century was in this world," said the Druid, unfolding one of the maps Sir Bedwyr had brought from the forest and spreading it over the kitchen table. "Sailing boats, long-distance trade in spices and silks. Horse-and-cart technology, but quite sophisticated even so." He pointed at a small, crescent-shaped island in the centre of the map, marked with a few towns and one port – Belhaven. "The Adamantine Sea touches Skarron about once every two years. It gives the merchants a chance to sell their goods to other worlds, and get some precious off-world luxuries as well. It's made Belhaven quite a thriving place."

Jem was staring at the map, tracing the outlines of several other islands and a mainland area with several large cities. It was labelled The Divided Kingdom.

"Divided?" he said. "How can you have a divided kingdom?"

"Civil war, about a hundred years back," said the Druid. "Nasty affair. Then they agreed to split, but both sides wanted the royal family. So they stayed one kingdom but the two halves are ruled by separate Grand Councils – made up of commoners in one half, and nobles in the other. The current king's just a ceremonial head. No real power over either half."

Inanna tossed her dark braids. "That is no way for a king to behave," she said. "I would have died rather than be a mere puppet ruler."

The Druid looked at her haughty expression and grinned. "I'm sure you would," he said. "In fact, the old king agreed with you – they had to chop his head off. His wife and children ran into exile, and it's the heirs of his younger brother who rule now."

Inanna's eyes widened in outrage. Cat couldn't help laughing. "We did the same to one of our kings, too," she said. "And they did it in France. Kings seem to get their heads chopped off quite regularly if they're not careful."

Inanna straightened her shoulders and put on her most regal expression. "When I am Empress of Ur-Akkad," she said loftily, "I shall ensure that the people love me too much to even *think* of chopping off my head!"

Jem exploded with laughter and she gave him a baleful look. "I'm sorry," he spluttered. "I'm sure they *will* love you! You're very… er… lovable. If a teensy bit bossy."

She narrowed her eyes at him, but before she could say anything, Sir Bedwyr was bowing before her with a flourish.

"O most glorious princess," he said, "your people will of course adore you. How could they do otherwise? They will be utterly in awe of your beauty and wit."

He straightened, his blue eyes gazing earnestly into her deep brown ones. Inanna, for once, was at a loss for words. Cat felt a slight twinge of jealousy, but then shrugged. Sir Bedwyr was extremely charming – it was no surprise if he was showering a little of that charm on an actual princess.

She turned to the Druid. "How do we get to this Belhaven place then?"

He rubbed his chin thoughtfully. "I've got an old friend who lives there. Local agent for the forest." He fished Albert Jemmet's keys out of the bowl where he'd thrown them. "We need to get to Albert's lock-up. If I'm not mistaken, he'll have a full set of agent's tokens there."

"Agent's tokens?" said Jem. "What are they?"

"Small objects – keys, jewellery. Things that retain a strong essence of the world they come from. We should be able to use the one for Belhaven to conjure a portal and find my friend." The Druid paused and contemplated them all seriously. "I'll go first. Check everything's safe. I'll come back for Cat and Inanna when I've made arrangements. Meanwhile they both need to get some practise at sensing and controlling objects."

He gestured towards Great-Aunt Irene, who was coming up the cellar stairs with a pile of dusty books in her arms.

"My old spell books," she said in triumph. "I *knew* I'd left them carefully stored somewhere! We'll have you sending your magic to objects in no time, don't worry!"

Cat and Inanna exchanged glances.

"Um, are you sure it's a good idea, going to Belhaven on your own?" said Cat. "Maybe if Inanna stayed, and I came and helped you…"

Inanna shot her a look of outrage. The Druid shook his head, smiling. "No, sorry, Cat. You really do need to get the hang of this magic. And so does Inanna."

"But I mastered the fire amber!" said Inanna crossly. "I'm sure I can do it again with another piece!"

Great Aunt Irene frowned. "It's not the same thing at all," she said. "For a start, the sea amber will almost certainly be bound to another heir. We can't guarantee they'll be cooperative. You'll need to be able to send your magic out to seek the jewel, find where it's hidden. And then if you do manage to steal it, you have to try and take control of a piece of amber that belongs rightly to another. That's very tricky. Only someone who's got a connection to one of the other pieces could even attempt such a thing, and even then, they need to know exactly what they're doing. Which is why you two –" she dumped the spell books down firmly on the kitchen table – "will be practising hard with me, and not gallivanting off to Belhaven till we're sure *exactly* where in the Adamantine Sea you need to be."

Inanna made a face, and threw herself into a chair.

Cat sighed. "OK," she said. "But you know, Uncle Lou, you really shouldn't be going on your own. I mean, can you even conjure a portal? It must be at least as difficult as a sugar bowl."

The Druid's face fell. "Damn," he said. "You're right. I'll have to take someone with me."

"I'll go," said Dora at once. "I can do the portal. And I know more magic than anyone else here."

"If Dora goes, I'm going," said Jem quickly. 'We're a team, aren't we, Dora?"

Dora rolled her eyes at him, but Cat could tell that she was pleased.

The Druid gave a theatrical sigh. "Well then, young Jem. It seems we'll be going to Belhaven in force. But no foolishness and no disobedience, or I'll turn you into a toad."

Jem raised one eyebrow and mouthed the words "sugar bowl".

The corner of the Druid's mouth twitched. "When I've got my strength back," he said. "And don't think I won't. A sludgy brown one with warts."

Sir Bedwyr stepped forward and gave the Druid a low bow. "Good luck!" he said, saluting the Druid with his sword. "Be assured I shall guard the Lady Catrin and Princess Inanna with my life."

Great-Aunt Irene sniffed. "I'm not sure that's necessary. But if you wish, you can start by patrolling the garden. And while you're there, you can do some pruning. The wisteria's got quite shocking since I died."

"Good," said the Druid. "Now we just need something to make a portal back from Belhaven." He looked round the kitchen with a small frown, and then his face cleared. "Aha!" he said. "This will do the trick." He picked up a small silver teaspoon from the sideboard. "I remember this from when Mother first moved here – must have been in this house twenty years at least. Should give us a good strong portal home." He tucked it in his pocket and then gestured to Dora and Jem. "Come along. We'll take Albert's motorbike. You can go on the back, Dora. I think we'll make Jem sit in the sidecar."

Cat followed them down the hallway and out of the front door. She watched as the Druid settled himself astride the battered old motorbike and kicked it into life. He, Jem and Dora put on the helmets that were piled in the sidecar and then he turned to her with a grin.

"We'll be back as soon as we can," he shouted over the noise of the engine. "Keep an eye on Inanna. Practise your magic. Don't do anything stupid."

Cat nodded. He gave her a thumbs up and then put the bike into gear. With a jolt, it pulled away, and Dora, startled, threw her arms round his waist and clung on. They roared down the road, leaving a cloud of black smoke behind them.

Cat felt hollow inside as she watched them go. First Simon, then Mum – now Uncle Lou. Everyone she cared about was disappearing, one after the other, leaving her to just wait and hope they would be all right. Hope that everything would work out.

She swallowed, and walked back down the hall to the kitchen. Tucking her short blonde hair behind her ears, she stood facing the ghost of Great-Aunt Irene.

"OK," she said. "How do I send my magic into an object?"

Chapter Six

Dora clung to the Druid's back as the motorbike accelerated down the road in a noisy cloud of fumes. She had never ridden on anything so disconcerting – not even the old rocking chair her grandmother had magicked to carry people round the village one summer fair. That had had a peculiar rolling motion and nine times out of ten deposited its passengers on their heads in the duck pond. But Albert Jemmet's motorbike was worse. Dora kept thinking she was going to slide off the back of it or get her feet trapped in the whirring wheels. Every time the Druid accelerated, the round metallic helmet she'd been given to wear pulled up under her chin and made her feel as if her head was going to be wrenched off. Out of the corner of her eye, she could see

Jem, leaning forward with excitement in the little oval carriage he was sitting in. He turned to her, his eyes shining.

"It's brilliant, Dora, isn't it?" he shouted.

"No! It's *awful!*" she shouted back, but the wind whipped her words away behind them as they slewed round a corner and the bike skidded to a halt outside Albert's garage.

The Druid dismounted and pulled off his helmet, running his fingers through his black hair with an expression of delight. "That was the most fun I've had in *years*," he said. "Such a shame I've never been able to get the internal combustion engine to work in the kingdom."

Dora removed her helmet and gingerly climbed off the back of the bike. The Druid laughed at her expression.

"Come on, Dora," he said encouragingly. "It's not that bad! A lot more reliable than a horse!"

Dora grimaced. "Horses," she said with feeling, "are a lot quieter. And a *lot* slower!"

Jem jumped out of the sidecar as the Druid opened the garage and together they pushed the bike into one corner and covered it with a tarpaulin. The Druid took a swift look round and then headed towards a cupboard at the back. It had a multitude of small drawers and on the shelves above were a whole array of little hooks with keys dangling from them. Each key had a hand-written label attached.

The Druid scanned the labels and pulled out a few drawers to check what was inside. Muttering under his breath, he rummaged through one of the drawers until he found a large metal ring, like a bangle, with a faded brown label.

"Catch!" he said, throwing it to Dora, who fumbled for it slightly but managed to stop it falling onto the floor. The ring was plain iron, the metal a little rusty. The label, in a bold italic hand, read: *Mooring ring, West Port, Belhaven: Isaac Drubel.*

"They're all from different worlds," said Jem, fingering a few of the keys and examining the attached labels. "But why keys?"

"Metal," said the Druid. "And a long association with a particular house. That makes them strong and accurate. Which is very useful when you need to get somewhere in a hurry."

"So metal's better for portals?" said Jem, interested. "Is that why you took the teaspoon? Because it's silver?"

The Druid nodded. "Metal holds the essence of a world better than any other material. And more importantly, it will forge a link to the particular bit of the world that it's been associated with longest. Cloth, on the other hand, is pretty well useless – your clothes absorb the essence of a new world almost instantly. No good trying to conjure a portal with your trousers."

"Have you ever tried?" said Jem, his eyes sparkling.

"I might have," said the Druid, looking faintly sheepish, and Dora stifled a laugh at the thought of the Druid, trouserless, frantically trying to make a portal to get away from a difficult situation.

"So what else works, apart from metal?" said Jem. "You used that railway ticket, so I guess paper…?"

"Not usually," said the Druid. "Unless it's got writing on it. Writing or printing is a powerful holder of a world's essence. Rubber's not too bad either – and glass is OK. But the best materials are metal or wood or stone. They're the three strongest components of a world's being. Damn near impossible to find in some worlds – everything's plastic. Plastic is *rubbish* for portals."

Jem took a plain iron key from the very first

hook on the board. "Hey!" he said. "This is from the kingdom!" He peered more closely at the label. "*The Outer Tap Room, Bull's Head Tavern, The Royal City*," he read, and then looked up. "Why would Albert want to go to the outer tap room of an inn in the city?"

"I can't think," said the Druid drily. "Perhaps when he wanted a quiet pint of kingdom beer and a chance to catch up with the gossip."

Jem grinned and twirled the key round his finger. "Right then, are we off? To this Belhaven place?"

The Druid turned to Dora. "Are you ready?' he said.

She nodded and fingered the mooring ring carefully. She could tell it came from another world. She closed her eyes, sensing a wet, cold place with the tang of salt in the air. There was very little of the spicy smell of magic that was found in the kingdom, but still, it didn't have quite the same flat, unmagical feel of Cat and Simon's world.

"There's a little magic there," she said, opening her eyes. "But it's strange – it doesn't feel like human magic."

"You're right, Dora," said the Druid with a

warm smile. "It's mostly nature magic in that world – water and river spirits, some tree people. Only a few humans can do magic, mostly from the Divided Kingdom. You're a remarkably strong witch, you know. Not many people would have picked that up."

Dora coloured at the praise, but she felt absurdly pleased. As she held the ring out in front of her, she noticed Jem quietly slipping the kingdom key he had found into his pocket. Dora frowned, but she didn't say anything. She was concentrating on feeling the other world the mooring ring came from, finding the gap between that world and this one, and inserting the twisty magic of the portal spell between them. As she said the words, a white mist swirled in front of them, and then solidified into a doorway. The Druid clapped one hand on Jem's shoulder and held out the other to Dora.

"Forward!" he said, and together they stepped through the mist.

Chapter Seven

Belhaven looked quite a lot like Dora had imagined it. They stepped out of the portal onto a wide stone quay, with boats in all sizes and states of disrepair leaning drunkenly against each other on the muddy sand or tied up against the harbour wall. Fishing nets and coils of rope were piled up by the quayside and seagulls wheeled overhead, screeching loudly. Everything smelled of fish.

Back from the quay, a row of timber-framed houses with narrow doors and windows peered disapprovingly across the harbour, their paint weathered and cracked, a few old lobster pots piled up by their front doors. The occasional window box of ragged sea pinks did nothing to brighten up their generally dour appearance. No one seemed to be about, which was lucky, as it meant their sudden arrival in the middle of the quayside drew no unwanted attention.

"This is the old port," said the Druid. "It's only used at high tide. The main commercial port is round the other side of the town. Come on!"

He set off with a long stride towards a narrow alley between two of the houses, but after a few paces had to stop and clutch his side.

"Sorry," he said, his face white. "Forgetting myself. Too fast. This blasted wound…"

"Lean on me," said Jem, offering his shoulder. The Druid put his hand on it gratefully.

"Give me a minute," he said. "I'll be fine."

Dora gently pulled his jacket aside and examined the place where Jones' spell had sliced into his side. She could see a stain of blood starting to seep across his shirt where the half-healed cut had opened up.

"Stand still," she said. "My grandmother taught me a spell that might help. I just need to modify it slightly."

She closed her eyes and felt for the right magic, then tweaked it a little and let it flow down from her fingertips. The Druid gasped and then straightened up, an expression of astonishment on his face.

"Worlds above, Dora! What did you do? It feels almost normal!"

Dora's eyes sparkled, but she tried to look nonchalant. She waved one hand airily. "Oh, you know. Just a little family secret…"

The Druid patted her on the back. "Whatever it was, it did the trick. I might even risk a spell or two when I've got over the shock. Well done!"

He set off again towards the passageway. As they followed, Jem leaned in to Dora and said, in a low voice, "What did you *do* to him?"

Dora glanced up at the Druid's back, and whispered out of the side of her mouth, "It's a spell my grandmother uses to mend leaking roofs. I changed it to work on skin."

Jem guffawed, and the Druid looked back with a quizzical expression. Both of them hurriedly caught up with him, trying to make themselves appear serious and ready for anything.

The narrow alley ran into a wider, more prosperous street, with tall stone houses lining each side. There were a few more people around now – bare-footed boys running errands or carrying boxes to or from the busy port, merchants in sober dark coats chatting to each other in doorways, or leaning over their balconies smoking a pipe and contemplating the morning bustle. The Druid stopped at a plain blue door with a brass knocker shaped like a dolphin. He rapped it smartly and after a few moments the door opened.

"The Druid to see Master Drubel," he said to the maidservant who answered. She bobbed a curtsey and disappeared. The next second a short, well-dressed man exploded out of the doorway and started pumping the Druid's arm up and down with enthusiasm. He had thick black hair and a square, cheerful face, and his bushy black eyebrows were shooting up and down as enthusiastically as his arm.

"My dear fellow! It's a delight – a marvel – to see you again! Why, it's been – what? – ten years? I can hardly believe it's you!"

"Isaac," said the Druid, pressing the man's hand warmly. "It is indeed me. And it's just as well my able apprentice here did a nifty bit of healing magic before we got here or you might just have killed me with that hearty welcome…"

"Healing magic?" said Isaac Drubel with a frown. "I can't believe you would let anyone past *your* guard, my dear Druid!"

"Smith and Jones," said the Druid, holding up his bandaged arm, and Isaac blanched.

"You'd better come in," he said, with a swift look left and right along the street. "Quickly. I had heard the crow karls were on the move. There have been rumours of them being seen in the Divided Kingdom – but I couldn't believe it. It's been such a long time since… Anyway, come in. Come in."

He gestured to the Druid to precede him into the hallway, and then ushered Jem and Dora in behind him. With another quick glance up and down the street, he followed them in and shut the door.

Isaac Drubel's house was crammed with all kinds of strange objects – statuettes, ornate vases, elaborately carved bowls. Curiosities and knick-knacks lined shelves and spilled over surfaces, and richly embroidered carpets in jewel-bright colours overlapped each other on every inch of floor. Isaac led them into a large sitting room with tall windows overlooking the street. He shifted a few teetering piles of boxes so they could get to the chairs by the fireplace.

"Apologies for the disorder," said Isaac as he heaved aside a mound of cloth with tiny mirrors embroidered on it. "My usual maid resigned a few days ago – the new one's not yet used to the system we have here."

The Druid laughed. He removed a slightly mouldy stuffed parrot from a cushioned stool and sat down. "System, Isaac? I've never known your house in anything but a state of complete chaos. I'm not sure you can call that a system."

Isaac shrugged apologetically. "You're probably right. But it's worse than usual. Even *I'm* not sure where everything is!"

The maid poked her head round the door.

"Would you be wanting any refreshments, Master Drubel?" she said. She had a rather pinched white face, and Dora noticed her sharp black eyes shooting from the Druid to Jem and back, as if memorising their appearance.

"No," said Isaac, waving his hand. "You get on. I know it's market day today, you're busy. I can see to my guests. They're old friends of mine."

"Very good, Master Drubel," said the maid, and with a last stare at Dora, she hurried off. A few moments later they heard the front door bang.

"Good," said Isaac. "That's got rid of her. Always sneaking around and lurking in doorways, that one. I'd sack her but I can't find anyone else. Since the Adamantine Sea connected with Skarron last week, the port's been busier than a nest of hornets. Everyone's working day and night to get the trade ships unloaded and get our goods off to sea. And we're having to contend with this blasted pirate now, of course."

"Pirate?" said Jem, his attention caught. "A real pirate?"

"Yes," said Isaac, his bushy black eyebrows coming together in a frown. "They've been plying the Adamantine Sea for a few years now. Picking off merchantmen from every port the sea touches. No one can chase them down. They have an uncanny ability to disappear in the middle of the sea."

"Do they now?" said the Druid, leaning forward. "And what might be the name of their ship?"

"The *Merryweather Mermaid*," said Isaac. "Why? Do you have any idea who they are?"

"No," said the Druid, rubbing his chin. "But I might have an inkling of how they're managing to disappear. We had word the sea amber was on a ship – I'd lay money it's this one. They're using the amber to dip in and out of worlds. It's a perfect set-up – you raid ports as they touch the Adamantine Sea, but when you're chased you can cross to another world and another bit of the sea."

"Yes, it fits," said Isaac. "But how in the forest's name did a piece of deep amber end up in the hands of a pirate?"

The Druid shrugged. "They got scattered. There are heirs all over the place. It's no stranger to find one captaining a pirate ship than – oh, I don't know – working as a computer games specialist just outside Basingstoke."

"What?" said Isaac, puzzled.

"Never mind," said the Druid with a grin, and pushed his unruly hair back off his face. "The important thing is, we need to get to this ship and we need to do it before Smith and Jones. Isaac, who's in port at the moment, and how fast are their ships?"

Chapter Eight

Jem was uneasy. Isaac Drubel's maid had struck him as rather untrustworthy. There was something about the expression on her face as she'd looked round at them all, and the hurried way she had left the house after they'd arrived, that struck him as suspicious. While the Druid and Isaac were bent over a map of Belhaven and the surrounding islands, deep in discussion about the possibility of chartering a ship, Jem sidled up to Dora and tapped her on the shoulder.

"I'm going to go and have a look around the town," he said in a low voice. "See if I can find the maidservant. There's something not quite right about her."

Dora glanced across at the Druid and then back at Jem. "I think you're right," she said with a worried expression. "But it could be dangerous. You don't know anything about the town. If Smith or Jones is here…"

"It's all right. I'll be careful. I'm good at blending in. I'll see you back here." He winked and clapped her on the shoulder, then slipped out of the room before she could protest any further.

When he reached the large front door, he opened it carefully and peered up and down the street. A few people were passing with packages and baskets, most of them heading up the street towards what appeared to be the centre of the small port town. Propping the door open, Jem sauntered out and made his way up the cobbled street, keeping a sharp eye out for Isaac Drubel's maid.

The town of Belhaven was a maze of rather crooked streets which twisted and turned between little cobbled squares, sometimes running steeply upwards, or crossing other streets on narrow stone bridges. Jem followed the general bustle and the smell of fish towards what he guessed must be the commercial harbour, looking out for Isaac's maid or the dark suits of Mr Smith or Mr Jones. But there was no sign of them.

Eventually the street he was in led into a larger square with a tavern and a couple of vegetable stalls. Three roads led off from the square. Two of them were little more than narrow alleyways, heading further up into the town, but the main thoroughfare ran straight and wide towards the harbour. Between the houses, Jem could see a broad expanse of white quay, glimpses of sparkling blue sea, and a jumbled forest of masts and rigging.

Just as he was about to set off towards the harbour, a movement caught his eye in one of the alleys. He paused and stepped sideways into the shadow of the tavern, bending over as if to retie one of his shoelaces. Peering through the fringe of red hair falling over his eyes, he could just make out a figure standing in the alley, apparently talking to someone in one of the narrow, ramshackle houses crowded in on either side. He squinted. It was hard to see, because the sun barely penetrated to the street level, but he thought the figure had the look of Isaac Drubel's maid. As he peered, she stepped up to the doorway of the house and disappeared inside it.

Jem stood up straight. He glanced around

quickly, but no one seemed in the least bit interested in him or what he was doing. Sticking his hands in his pockets and trying to look casual, he strolled into the alley and headed for the place where he thought the maid had been standing.

The alley was dark and smelled of seaweed. The houses on either side were run down, their paint peeling, their windows grimy or boarded over. Dark scummy water ran down channels either side of the street or spilled over it where the channels were blocked with rubbish and decaying bits of net. Jem hesitated in front of what he thought was the right door. His heart was thumping loudly in his chest and his mouth felt dry. A coldness seemed to emanate from the house, as if it were in deeper shadow than the rest of the alley. The door was cracked, its edges splintered with rot and a small round window in the middle was like a dark eye looking back at him. Lying below it on the doorstep was a single crow's feather.

Jem stared at it for a moment. Smith or Jones had been here – possibly they were still in the house. He had no magic, unlike Dora. He didn't even have the short sword he usually carried with him everywhere – it had been confiscated in Cat and Simon's world. He had nothing with which to protect himself.

Jem knew he should just return to Isaac Drubel's house – tell the Druid what he'd seen. It would be the safest and most sensible option. But Jem didn't like playing safe. Where was the fun in that? And if he wanted to be a forest agent, he'd have to be prepared to deal with the allies of the dark, magic or no magic. He had his wits, he had his agility, and, as the Druid was always telling him, he had been blessed with an almost endless supply of foolhardiness. He glanced up and down the alley. No one was about. He looked sideways at an old barrel standing up against the wall of the house, and measured the distance from the top of the barrel to the first-floor balcony. Taking a deep breath, he made his decision.

Jem jumped up onto the barrel, stood up straight and, rocking on his heels, launched himself at the lower edge of the balcony. He managed to grab hold of one of the struts that supported it, and quickly brought his feet up, wedging them firmly into the wooden structure. Then he pulled himself up, hand over foot, until he was straddling the top rail of the balcony. He paused, and listened. No sound came from the house or the street below – no shout of alarm or thump of feet running. Carefully he shifted his weight and slipped fully over the balcony rail, then ducked down against the double doors that led into the house. He peered through the narrow gap between the doors. The room behind was empty and dark. Holding his breath, he pressed his hands against the doors and felt them move. They weren't locked.

Jem eased the two doors apart and slipped into the room, treading as softly as a cat. There was just light enough to see a rather plain wooden bed and a thin rug on the floor. A jug of water stood by a cracked porcelain bowl on a cupboard next to the bed, and flung on the bed, as if it had been thrown off in a hurry, was a voluminous grey nightshirt with ragged edges.

Jem relaxed slightly. He was pretty sure neither Mr Smith nor Mr Jones would ever be found in such a nondescript and threadbare garment. That's if they even changed to go to sleep. He couldn't imagine either of them sleeping in anything other than their shiny black suits. Come to think of it, he couldn't really imagine them lying in a bed at all. Did they just perch on a roof beam somewhere, one beady black eye open at all times? Jem shivered and found himself looking up at the ceiling – but it was just plain white plaster. No beams, no dark-suited crow men.

Jem tiptoed to the door of the bedroom and put his eye to a large crack in the wood. No one appeared to be on the other side, but he could hear the drifting murmur of voices from downstairs. He carefully opened the door and crept out onto the landing. Floating up the stairwell were the sharp tones of Isaac Drubel's maid, interspersed with a deeper, male voice. He froze for a moment, but it was neither the slightly nasal twang of Mr Smith nor the dry, dusty voice of Mr Jones. It was deeper, rougher, and punctuated with loud yawns. Jem craned over the rather rickety banisters.

"…you great lolloping nitwit, they'll use your guts to rig the ship if you don't get it seaworthy by tonight. They leave on the tide, at sunset, they said. And here's you – lying on your back inhaling flies!"

"Yeah, well…" came the rumbling reply, interrupted by a yawn. "Up till the poxing small hours rounding up a crew, weren't I? Every tardy landlubber with one leg's got a berth on the merchant ships now the Sea's in…"

"Rats to your excuses, Henry. Get down there and fix the ship or you're no brother of mine! You'll be less good to me than a pig's behind by the time they've finished with you! And…" She lowered her voice, and Jem could only just hear the odd word of what she was saying. "…Master Drubel… come in… need… forest…"

Jem leaned over further, straining his ears. He still couldn't quite catch her words. Maybe if he just shifted his weight a little, got his head down lower…

Crack!

A rotten banister snapped in two and the whole structure shifted. Jem was catapulted over the rail and, legs and arms flailing, he hit the wooden floor below with a terrific thud.

The fall knocked all the wind out of him, but it was a low-ceilinged house and apart from a gash above his right eye, he was unhurt. Standing over him was a huge man with a red beard. He was wearing a grubby white shirt and black breeches, with a grimy red neckerchief round his bull-like neck. He looked sleepy and confused, as if he'd just got out of bed.

Jem opened and shut his mouth like a stranded fish, trying to force some air back into his lungs, but just as he managed to take a breath, the man pounced. Grabbing Jem round the waist he hauled him up bodily, wrapping a meaty arm round Jem's neck and pulling hard. Jem struggled and kicked but the man just tightened his grip.

"Any more of that an' I'll just squeeze a bit more, see?"

Jem stopped, and the man turned so he was facing Isaac Drubel's maid.

"Who's this little ratsbane, then, Eliza?" he said. "Poxing spy?"

Eliza's eyes narrowed as she looked Jem up and down. "It's the boy from Drubel's house. He must have followed me."

"Shall I kill him?" said the large man.

Jem held his breath. The woman considered. "Best not," she said. "They might want to talk to him. But I need to get back – and you need to get the ship ready…"

She put her face close to Jem's, her expression cold.

"You'll be sorry for this," she said. "You should've stayed safe at home."

Jem looked into her black eyes and saw something of the same dark malevolence he'd recognised in Smith and Jones. He felt a coldness build up through his body and thought, *She's spelling me! I need to do something, quickly!*

With a sudden movement that took his captor by surprise, Jem arched his back and smashed his head into the big man's chest, then bent down and sank his teeth into his brawny arm. The man yelled and loosened his grip just enough for Jem to slip out from under it. Launching himself across the room, he fended Eliza off with one arm and crashed out of the front door into the alley. Without looking back, he hurtled up the alley and twisted sideways into one of the narrow streets, hoping he could find his way back to Isaac Drubel's house before Eliza or her brother could catch him. He had to get to the Druid and Dora. He had to warn them. Smith and Jones were already in Belhaven – and what was worse, they would very soon know the Druid was there too. And exactly where to find him.

Chapter Nine

Dora was in an agony of impatience. Jem had been gone for what felt like hours, and the Druid and Isaac were no nearer to working out a plan for getting on board the *Merryweather Mermaid*. Most of the port's fastest ships were already chartered, or had left when the Adamantine Sea first touched Belhaven. Isaac thought that they should simply take passage on one of the merchant ships, hope to be boarded by the pirates, but the Druid wasn't convinced.

"It's too risky. And too slow. Smith and Jones are after the amber and for all we know they've already tracked it down to this corner of the Adamantine Sea. No – there's only one thing for it. We need to ask Leeven for help."

Isaac turned two shades paler.

"Leeven?" he said. "Are you sure? After last time?"

The Druid pulled at his ear. "We've always been on friendly terms," he said, but Dora thought there was something a little guarded in his tone. Then he shrugged and grinned. "I don't think he'll bear a grudge over one little misunderstanding. But there's only one way to find out, eh?"

Isaac looked dubious, but he nodded. "A tributary runs through my garden," he said. "We can call him there."

The Druid stood up, then looked round the room with a frown. "Dora? Where's Jem?"

Dora bit her lip. "He left right after we got here – went to follow your maid, Master Drubel. I'm – I'm a bit worried about him. He should have been back ages ago."

The Druid raised an eyebrow at Isaac. "Your maid... Does she by any chance come from the Divided Kingdom?"

Isaac frowned. "Gullvast. Why?"

"There was something about her. A whiff of magic. I wonder...?"

"I think we need to get after Jem," said Dora, controlling her voice with difficulty. A terrible feeling that they were in danger – that Jem was in danger – was building up inside her till she thought she might scream. "Please – I think he's in trouble."

The Druid hesitated, then cursed. "All right, Dora. You come with me. Isaac – can you get to your garden, start the invocation? If Jem –"

But at that moment the door slammed open and Jem himself appeared, breathing hard, his eyes wild. A trickle of blood ran down his cheek from a gash on his forehead.

"The... the..." he panted, pointing back behind him. "Eliza... after me..." He stopped to catch his breath and then blurted out, "Your maid, Master Drubel. She's working with Smith and Jones. Her brother's fitting out a ship for them. They're going to tell them we're here!"

All the tension of the last hour of waiting seemed to rise up inside Dora and she threw herself at Jem and started pummelling him with her fists. "You idiot! You shouldn't have followed her! You could have got caught! You could have got *killed*! I thought you *had*..."

Jem looked startled and grabbed her wrists. "It's all right, Dora," he said, in a soothing tone.

"I'm fine. Well, mostly fine. You could do a bit of roof-mending magic on my forehead, if you like." He put one hand up to his head, and showed her the blood on his fingers with a grin.

Dora looked at his crooked, freckled face and felt a mixture of relief that he was here, alive, in front of her, and exasperation that he insisted on flinging himself into any danger he could find and yet somehow managed to come out unharmed and looking pleased with himself. She gave him another punch, hard, on the arm, and he laughed.

"I *did* get caught," he admitted. "I thought I was done for – Eliza's a magic user. She nearly froze me solid."

The Druid and Isaac exchanged glances and the Druid turned to Jem. "Are they following you?"

"They ran after me to start with," said Jem, "but I think I lost them in all the maze of streets. I lost myself, come to that. It's a good half-hour since I escaped. One of them's bound to have gone to Smith and Jones by now."

Isaac Drubel made his way hurriedly to the front door. Checking left and right down the street, he shut it with a bang and slotted an iron bar across it, muttering a few words as he did so.

"That might hold them for a few moments," he said.

The Druid looked grim. "If your maid's working for them, Isaac, then moments is probably all we've got. We need to call Leeven – and we need to do it now."

"We'd better get down to the garden," said Isaac, and gestured for them to follow him down the long hallway. The Druid strode after him, and Jem turned to Dora.

"What was all that about?" he said.

She shook her head. The Druid was obviously intent on calling on someone for help – a rather important someone, from Isaac's response. But she had a feeling that this someone might not have an entirely positive relationship with the Druid. And she had no idea who – or what – the someone was going to turn out to be.

The Druid was leaning over the bank of a small stream at the bottom of Isaac Drubel's garden, his unbandaged right hand held just under the surface of the water. He was frowning in concentration, his eyes closed, his lips moving, but the words of the spell he was intoning were so faint Dora could barely hear them. She could see beads of sweat on his forehead, and she was rather worried that at any moment he was going to faint and topple head first into the water. Jem was obviously of the same opinion, because he moved forward and stood over the Druid as if ready to catch him when he fell.

At first nothing seemed to be happening. *He hasn't got enough magic*, thought Dora, and she glanced anxiously at the house behind them. But then she noticed a bubbling in the water around the Druid's hand. The stream seemed to be pooling, its flow through the garden interrupted. Water was gathering in front of the Druid, stirring and boiling, tumbling up from below the surface and coalescing in front of him. It was like watching clay take shape on a potter's wheel, the water whirling round and up until the entire stream had gathered itself into the shape of a man looming above them.

They all took a step backwards as the man bent down and looked at them. He was tall, with flowing hair and beard. His face was utterly solid, as if chiselled out of glass. His features were sharp, his expression cold. The lower part of his body was less formed, flowing and dancing as the water swirled round what looked sometimes like legs, sometimes like a fish's tail. *It's a river spirit*, thought Dora, feeling breathless.

"You!" the man said to the Druid, his brows knitted. His voice was like the roar of a waterfall. "You dare call me again? I owe you *nothing*!"

The Druid held up his hands in acknowledgement. "Of course. Just so. Nothing. But if you could see your way to one more favour. We need –"

But he got no further. The man reached out a hand and the Druid was sucked into a whirlpool of water, thrown up way above their heads and then dangled upside-down from one of the man's fingers. He laughed, with a sound like a wave crashing on a pebbly shore. "Little Druid," he said, gloating. "You were warned, last time. Your trickery bought you three favours, and I've given them to you. But now – now, I can *enjoy* myself!"

Chapter Ten

The man of water crooked his finger and the Druid spun round several times, his long legs flailing. When the rotations stopped he was at least dangling the right way up, but Dora could see that he'd gone a pale shade of green. Dora glanced at Isaac. He looked terrified and was clearly unable to do anything to help. Jem had his mouth open and seemed rooted to the spot. Dora stepped up to the edge of the stream and smacked her hand into the wall of water in front of her.

"Stop it!" she shouted. "I don't know what the Druid did last time he was here and I don't care. Right now, there are two agents of the dark in Belhaven. You need to help us stop them or –" she hesitated, unsure how much she could reveal to this river spirit – "or I don't know *what* might happen – but probably something horrible!"

Jem winced, and Dora gave him an anguished look. Even to her, the warning sounded pretty lame, but it was the best she could do. The man turned his gaze on Dora, and she tried hard to outstare him. She fixed him with her fiercest expression, the one she used on her unruly boy cousins when they interrupted her spell practice.

There was a rumble from the man, and then the Druid was replaced gently on the riverbank, where he staggered slightly and was sick. The wall of water reduced in height till the man's face was level with Dora's, his expression amused.

"Well, little witch," he said. "Bravely spoken. I wouldn't have hurt him, you know. Just given him a little – well, let's just say I owe him payback for something." He rumbled with laughter and then flicked a finger at the Druid, who was bent over with his hands on his knees. A small tidal wave was dropped onto the Druid's head, plastering his hair to his face and soaking his clothes. The Druid stood up, and wiped his hair away from his forehead.

"Thanks, Dora," he said. "I owe you. Twice."

The man leaned over again towards Dora. "So. Did you say *agents of the dark*?"

"Yes," she said. "Smith and Jones. They're working for Lord Ravenglass, from our world."

"Then you did right to call me," said the man sternly. "The river Leeven has always been an enemy of the dark. How can I help?"

"The *Merryweather Mermaid*," said the Druid, moving closer. "Do you know the ship?"

Leevan looked thoughtful. "I do," he rumbled. "They anchored in the bay several days ago. Pirates, the merchants call them. But they are friends to the shore folk. What they take from the merchants, they share freely with the wharf rats, the fishers and the dockers. And they keep to the old religion. I will not see them harmed."

"We don't seek to harm them," said the Druid. "But they have something we need. Something we have to get before the agents of the dark find it."

Leevan stroked his beard. "It's the sea amber, then, that you are after," he stated. "I've felt them use its magic."

"Yes," said the Druid. "Ravenglass wants it to remake the amber crown. To release Lukos."

"*Lukos*," said Leevan, and his voice was like a

heavy downpour on a grey day. "I would not wish to see him at large in the world again. I will do whatever I can."

"We need to get to the ship as soon as possible," the Druid said. "She was anchored in your waters. Somewhere on your estuary bed there might be some part of the ship – a nail, a rotten bit of planking... If you could locate such a thing, we could make a portal."

"And – er – if you could see your way to doing that quite soon," said Isaac Drubel, glancing anxiously behind him at the house. "The agents of the dark might be here any moment."

Leeven frowned, his eyes as dark and cold as a stormy sea, and the water that formed his body churned fiercely. Dora could see that the Druid and Isaac had got it all wrong. Leeven was not just a river spirit, he was clearly a sort of god in his world. You might rail and shout at a god, or plead for help, but you didn't just tell him what to do. Leeven was clearly offended – and he was on the verge of showing them just exactly what gods did when they were offended.

She stepped forward and bowed deeply.

"Please," she said. "We need you. You're our only

hope to stop the dark. To save the worlds of light."

Leeven harrumphed, but his expression softened. Jem, catching on, threw himself down on his knees next to Dora.

"Great river," he said, "we beseech you…"

Dora frowned and flapped her hand at him to shut up. *Trust Jem to overdo it*, she thought.

But before he could say another word there was a tremendous explosion from behind them. They turned in time to see every window and door in Isaac Drubel's house shatter into a thousand pieces. A force like a hurricane expanded across the garden, throwing them all off balance. The next moment, the back wall of the house had collapsed into rubble, and standing in the middle of it were two tall, thin men in black suits.

"A meeting of old friends," said Mr Smith in his stretched voice. His black eyes were like stones. As he reached out one hand, Dora felt a tightening around her throat, and realised with a sense of panic that she couldn't breathe. Next to her, Jem had gone red and was making choking sounds, while Isaac Drubel had just keeled over and passed out on the grass. The Druid was trying to speak, but Mr Jones was almost on him, one claw-like hand poised to clasp him on the shoulder. Both of them ignored the man of water – it was as if they couldn't see him standing there in front of them.

The river man reached out one enormous hand. He scooped Mr Jones up, and then threw a mighty wave at Mr Smith, sluicing him down the garden and into the stream. Both the crow men were soon spinning round in deep whirlpools, unable to speak or free themselves, their spells shattered. Dora took a great breath, and heard Jem next to her wheezing, his face gradually returning to a normal colour.

"I'll take them down to the estuary with me," Leeven rumbled. "And I'll see how many bits of matchwood I can turn their ship into. But these vermin can't be killed by such as me, more's the pity."

The Druid bowed. "We are grateful," he said, massaging his neck. "And... apologies. For last time."

Leeven laughed. "You owe me, little Druid," he said. "But if you stop Lukos, count your debt paid."

Turning Smith and Jones round a few more times in a spinning whirlpool, Leeven folded in on himself, his shape dissolving into a huge wave which went crashing down onto the stream bed. The rolling, boiling torrent of water flowed down the channel, dragging the two dark figures with it.

Just as they disappeared, a stray wave rose up in the streambed and splashed down in front of Dora. As the water flowed back down the bank, it revealed a large black nail in the grass at her feet.

Dora picked it up, and the Druid clapped her on the back with a grin.

"That," he said, "would be a planking nail. And if I'm not mistaken, it's from the *Merryweather Mermaid*. Well done, Dora! He must have liked you."

Isaac groaned and sat up, rubbing his head. "What…?" he said. And then he saw his house and groaned again. "Pox," he said.

"Yes, well, sorry abut that," said the Druid cheerfully. "But we got what we came for. And Smith and Jones have been nicely delayed. Now we just need to get back and see about sending Cat and Inanna to the *Mermaid*."

Isaac pulled himself to his feet and sighed as he contemplated the rubble in his garden.

"Ah, well," he said. He nodded at Dora and Jem, and clasped the Druid's arm. "Good luck," he said. "And the forest's blessings go with you."

For a moment, the Druid held his gaze. "Thanks," he said quietly. "We'll need them, I'm sure, before the end."

He turned to Dora and handed her Great-Aunt Irene's teaspoon. "Portal, Dora, quick as you can," he said. "We have to get back to Wemworthy. We've got a job to do. And we have considerably less time to do it than I'd hoped."

Chapter Eleven

The smoke alarm above the kitchen table was shrieking like an express train, while Inanna held her hands over her ears and added her own squeals to the noise. Cat jumped up on the table and flapped at the alarm with a newspaper until it finally spluttered into silence. Then she turned to Inanna, hands on her hips.

"So help me, Inanna, if you do that again, I swear I'll lock you in the cellar till Uncle Lou comes back!"

Inanna covered her face with her hands and wailed. "I can't help it! Every time I send my magic into anything it bursts into flames."

Inanna had been practising on a small wooden bowl. Great-Aunt Irene drifted over and inspected the burned remains. "You're getting it to do *something*, at least," she said. "But perhaps you should continue in the garden. The table is looking rather… well… scorched."

It was true. There was a large black patch in the centre of it, and sooty marks on the ceiling above – although, thought Cat, some of those might have been from the time she and Simon had tried to open Great-Aunt Irene's enchanted box by setting fire to it with half a bottle of brandy.

Cat sighed and climbed down off the table. "Maybe you *should* try the garden, Inanna. Sir Bedwyr could stand by with a bucket of water."

Inanna sniffed, and Cat patted her on the back. "At least your magic's having an effect," she said. "I can't seem to get the hang of it at all."

"It's not much use though, is it?" said Inanna dolefully. "We find the amber and I immediately set fire to the ship."

"You won't be setting fire to the ship, Inanna," said Great-Aunt Irene in disapproval, "because if you can't get a little more control of your magic, you won't be going at all. Now get along outside, and practise on these egg cups."

She handed Inanna three china egg-cups from the nearby shelf, and then winked at Cat.

"Present from my older sister," she said. "Never liked them."

Inanna gave a faint half-smile and Great-Aunt Irene pushed her gently out of the back door. "You're meant to be sending a *little bit* of magic into the object, Inanna," she called after her. "It's not the same thing at all as doing a spell on it. Don't try so hard!"

She shut the back door, and then turned her beady silvery eyes on Cat.

"Now then. You're closer than you think, Cat. You're beginning to sense objects. What you have to do now is just send a small thread of magic out to them. You just want a connection. Nothing more."

Cat closed her eyes in concentration. She had started by working on sensing things, and she'd discovered that she was quite good at it. With a clear picture in her mind of the object she was looking for, a pottery vase, she'd been able to extend her senses outwards, across the room, even down the corridor, till she'd felt it snag her consciousness. But getting to the next stage – making a connection with the vase, sending her magic to it – was driving her to despair.

"I can't!" she said, opening her eyes. "I don't know how! I don't know what to do!"

Great-Aunt Irene moved behind her and took hold of her shoulders. Cat could feel her faint, icy touch on the sides of her neck.

"Remember when you undid Ravenglass's spells on the earth amber?" she said. "You saw his spells through my eyes, as threads of silver. Your own magic is the same. Picture it in front of you. Send it to the place where you know the vase is. Just a little thread, Cat. Not a whole spell. Just a connection."

Cat kept her eyes open and felt for the magic inside her. She pushed a little, sending it outwards, and then gasped as she saw a faint silvery wisp materialise in the air in front of her. Pushing more, she sent the wisp floating across the room towards the door. Behind it a trail of silver remained, anchoring it to where she was standing. The thread of silver extended further, till she felt it settle on the vase in the hall.

Cat gasped. Suddenly it was as if the vase was just a hair's breadth from her hand. She could have reached out, touched it, toppled it from the table it was siting on. Even – she almost giggled – set it on fire.

"Excellent!" said Great-Aunt Irene. She removed her hands from Cat's shoulders and the silvery thread disappeared. But then Cat shifted something in her mind and it reappeared, not silvery now but faintly purple.

"I can see it again!" she exclaimed.

"You're seeing it with your own spell sight," said Great-Aunt Irene in approval. "Well done, Cat! I knew you'd do it. You're easily the best pupil I've had. Louis took months to learn that!"

Cat glowed. She pulled back the thread of magic and then, just to see if she could, she sent it to a fruit bowl on the sideboard. Nudging with her mind, she pushed an apple off the top of the pile and helped it roll across the surface to her waiting hand. She picked it up, threw it in the air, and caught it in triumph.

"Now I just have to hope I can do it with the amber!" she said.

Great-Aunt Irene looked thoughtful. "It will be trickier. It's got magic of its own, and it will have a connection to whoever owns it. But the principle is the same. You'll just have to do your best."

Cat was playing with sending her magic from the

vase in the hallway to the lamp in the living room, when a faint white mist started to materialise in the corner of the kitchen. Almost immediately the portal solidified and Dora, Jem and the Druid stumbled through.

"Uncle Lou!" said Cat. "You've been ages! What happened?" She could see the Druid was drenched with water and both Dora and Jem looked rather stunned.

"It's a bit complicated," said the Druid. "Can someone hand me a towel?"

Cat handed him one of the drying-up cloths, and he bent over and started rubbing his hair vigorously.

"No time for long explanations," he said as he rubbed his head. "Smith and Jones are in Belhaven, but an old friend of mine has had words with them. Should take them at least a day to recover from the conversation. So we're ahead of the game. And thanks to Dora, we have a way of making a portal to the *Merryweather Mermaid*, where the amber's to be found."

He stood upright with a grin. "We ought to go now – no time to lose. I'll need you, Cat, and possibly Inanna, and..." He frowned, and then put out one hand as if to steady himself. "Er… actually, I feel a bit…" he said, and then he slowly toppled over onto the floor.

"Uncle Lou!" cried Cat in alarm.

Jem knelt down, lifted the Druid's head and shook him slightly. The Druid opened his eyes, looking confused.

"What – what happened? Am I *on the floor*?" he said, surprised.

"You fainted," said Jem. "Went down with an awful crash. Do you feel OK?"

The Druid felt the back of his head and groaned. He started to sit up, but then grimaced, and lay back down again. "I'll be all right," he said. "Give me a minute." He closed his eyes, and Jem looked over at Dora with a worried expression.

"It's the stab wound," he said. "I know you patched him up on the outside, Dora, but being tumbled upside down can't have been good for him."

"Upside down?" said Cat. "Who tumbled him upside down?"

"Leeven," said Dora. "He's a river spirit. They'd had some kind of disagreement, but they made it up. He's the one who gave us this." She held out her hand and Cat could see a large black nail lying on her palm. "It's a nail from the *Merryweather Mermaid*. It should give us a portal to the ship."

"Or thereabouts," said the Druid in a faint voice, his eyes still closed.

"Thereabouts?" said Cat. "What's that supposed to mean?"

Great-Aunt Irene drifted over to Dora's side. "It's a planking nail, is it not, my dear?" she said. Dora nodded. "Well, it will take us very close to where the nail was embedded in the ship's planking. But that could mean either side of the hull. In the ship's hold – or in the water."

Cat sat down on one of the kitchen chairs.

"So we've got a way to get to the ship. But Uncle Lou's in no fit state to go anywhere. It will have to be me. And maybe one of the rest of you. Jem, could you go and get Sir Bedwyr and Innana from the garden? And while you're at it, you'd better ask if either of them can swim."

Chapter Twelve

It was Dora who had the bright idea of conjuring a portal just to check whether the nail did indeed take them to the seaward side of the boat. She conjured it in the corner of the kitchen, just across from where the Druid was now sitting propped in an armchair.

Jem stuck his head through the misty doorway, gurgled, and pulled it back again. His red hair was plastered to his freckled face and water was running in rivulets down his neck.

"Yep," he said. "Definitely underwater."

"Damn," said the Druid.

"Well, that's that, then," said Great-Aunt Irene briskly. "You can't possibly go, Lou. Not if it involves treading water for several minutes and hoping to be rescued by a bunch of pirates. Cat's going to have to take one of the others."

"I'll go," said Jem.

Sir Bedwyr put his hand on his sword hilt and stood up straight. "I would defend you to the death, Lady Catrin," he said. "But alas, I cannot swim."

"Neither can I," said Dora apologetically. "I never learned."

"I can swim fine," said Jem.

Inanna stepped forward hesitantly.

"Should I go?" she said. "I can swim. I haven't exactly mastered the sending magic yet – but I have got better at it. Haven't I, Sir Bedwyr?"

The knight coughed and shuffled his feet. "Well, er, yes. Yes. The last one was only a very *tiny* fire…" he said, with an apologetic glance at Inanna.

"You need to stay here, Inanna," said Great-Aunt Irene. "Practise your magic more."

Jem rolled his eyes.

"I can go. *And* I can swim," he said again.

The Druid grimaced, and sat a little more upright. "Unfortunately – Forest help us – it looks like it *is* going to have to be young Jem here that goes. He's the best swimmer, and he's probably the best at talking his way out of a sticky situation."

"Jem it is, then," said Cat. "But I'll need something to make a portal to come back."

The Druid dug the silver teaspoon out of one of his pockets and held it out to her. Then, almost as an afterthought, he took out the golden-yellow leaf Albert had given him. "If you're in danger," he said, "use this. It's quicker than a portal – just needs a simple spell word." He gestured for her to bend closer and whispered the word in her ear. Cat nodded and tucked the leaf in her jeans pocket.

Great-Aunt Irene rapped her cane on the floor. "Excellent," she said. "We just need to think of a convenient story for them suddenly appearing in the middle of the sea. And it might be sensible if they have something to eat before they go. Pirate ship rations are generally rather nasty. They have weevils in them."

Dora sat at the kitchen table, thinking, while Inanna and Sir Bedwyr raided the cupboards for food. If Jem was going to the Adamantine Sea with Cat, then that left her here with nothing to do except wait for news. Dora felt restless, and there was a nagging anxiety pressing at the back of her mind. They had a head start on Smith and Jones, it was true, but was it going to be enough? And what was happening in the kingdom? Florence and Albert had been in the city for hours now, but there'd been no news of them. Had they managed to get to Simon? Had they been caught? She wondered whether Simon was still under Lord Ravenglass's spell, or whether he'd thrown it off. And if he had, would Ravenglass bother to put him under another spell, or would he just kill him?

Dora shivered. She felt rather responsible for Simon. She'd taught him portal magic when she probably shouldn't have done. She'd encouraged him to try to get to the kingdom. And then he'd met Lukos and been dragged into Ravenglass's plans.

The others bustled into the kitchen, and Jem plonked himself down next to Dora. The pile of food on the table started to diminish as everyone grabbed bits of bread, ham and fruit. Dora took a bread roll and started to chew it absently, but she wasn't feeling particularly hungry.

"Jem," she said in a low tone, "have you still got that key from Albert's lock-up?"

He turned to her in surprise. "You saw me take it?" he said.

Dora just looked at him, and he grinned. "Yes, I've still got it. Why?"

She gestured for him to follow her, then slipped out of the kitchen and down the hallway to the front room. A few minutes later, she heard Jem announce in a cheery voice that he had to go and use the flushing machine, and he came down the hallway after her. Leaning against the door of the lounge, he folded his arms and raised his eyebrows.

"So, what's up?" he said.

"I'm worried about Simon," she said. "There's been no word from Florence and Albert. We should have heard something by now. I was thinking… While you go to the Adamantine Sea, maybe I should go to the palace. Look for Simon."

Jem looked thoroughly taken aback. "On your own?" he said. "You're thinking of going to find him by yourself?"

Dora frowned at him. "I am capable of doing things on my own, you know, Jem Tollpuddle," she said tartly.

He raised his hands in mock surrender. "OK, don't spell me. It's just... Lord Ravenglass is there. And it sounds as if this Lukos character is lurking somewhere in the cellars. It's too dangerous, Dora!"

She bit her lip. "I don't like the idea of running into Lord Ravenglass again. He gives me the creeps. But we should have heard from Albert and Florence by now. I've got a bad feeing about it. I think someone needs to go there and find out what's happened."

"Shouldn't we tell the others?" said Jem.

"No," said Dora quickly. "They'll insist it's too dangerous, or make Sir Bedwyr go with me – and it's better if it's just me. I'm much more inconspicuous on my own." She tried to grin, but she didn't think she'd been very successful. Jem was looking at her with an odd expression on his face. She gave him a punch on the arm. "Anyway, I'm not going to sit here and do nothing while you and Cat are off on a pirate ship!"

Jem contemplated her for a moment. He seemed about to say something, but then he thought better of it. Eventually he shrugged.

"OK. I'll get the sea amber, and you can go

and get Simon." He fished in his pocket for the plain iron key and handed it to her. Then, after a moment's hesitation, he gave her a fierce hug, squashing her face into the scratchy wool of his jumper and resting his chin on the top of her head.

"Take care, Dora," he said. "Take really good care."

When Jem got back to the kitchen, the Druid looked up at him with a frown.

"Did I feel portal magic a moment ago?" he said.

Jem nodded. He looked a little shocked, Cat thought. As if he'd realised something utterly surprising.

"Dora," he said. "She's gone to the kingdom. To see if she can help rescue Simon."

Cat's mouth fell open. "Dora?" she said. "She went on her own?"

The Druid looked worried. "I think she's right," he said. "Someone does need to check what's happening in the kingdom. But I wish she had one of us with her."

"Dora's a fine witch," said Great-Aunt Irene.

"She'll be all right. And the best thing we can do for her now is get on with finding the sea amber."

Cat stood up, holding the planking nail. "Time to go, then," she said to Jem.

Inanna came over and gave her a hug. "I'm sorry, Cat," she said, her lip wobbling slightly. "I should have mastered the magic. Then I could have helped."

Cat grinned. "Don't worry, Inanna. Someone needs to stay and look after Uncle Lou, anyway – and I'm sure you'll be much better at that than Jem would be."

Inanna brightened. "Oh, yes! Of course I can do that! I know some healing from working in the temple sanctuary. I can make him a poultice from boiled leaves, and a strengthening broth. I'm sure I saw some cabbages in the vegetable basket when we were getting lunch."

The Druid made a face. "Erm, thanks, Inanna. But maybe you'd better carry on practising your magic. I'm feeling… just fine, actually. No poultices necessary."

Inanna pouted. "I will make you a poultice and *then* I will practise my magic!" she said firmly.

Jem grinned. "Looks like you're in excellent

hands," he said to the Druid. "Right, Cat. Portal. And maybe we'd better take off our shoes."

Cat held out the black nail and said the words of the portal spell. A misty doorway materialised in the kitchen, and she stuck her hand into it. There was definitely water the other side, but at least it was relatively warm. She unlaced her boots and tucked them under the kitchen table, wondering how long it would be before she'd be back to claim them. Or if she ever would.

Swallowing hard, she watched Jem dive head first through the portal, and then, taking a deep breath, she followed him.

Chapter Thirteen

In the outer tap room of the Bull's Head tavern, a white, misty portal had just materialised. The room was at the end of a long corridor, well away from the busy parts of the inn, and it didn't contain much apart from empty barrels of wine and ale, and a few old broken tables. So when Dora, still clutching Albert's dusty key, slipped out of the portal and into the room, there was no one to see her.

She pushed open the back door of the tap room and peered out. There was a small cluttered yard outside, and off it a narrow alley led to one of the main streets of the Royal City. As with everywhere in the city, she could see the tops of the palace towers, gleaming white in the sunlight and looming over the jumbled red roofs of the houses below. Dora breathed in the smell – pigs and rotting vegetables and the spicy tang of magic – and felt at home for the first time in days.

She wondered what the best thing was to do, now she was here. She had no idea where Albert or Florence might be, or how Albert had planned to get into the palace. She probably ought to just try and find Simon, she thought. If something had happened to the others, then Simon still needed rescuing. And if they were fine and on their way to him, they would all meet up eventually.

Looking round the tap room, Dora spotted a pile of grimy aprons thrown haphazardly across a bench. She could try getting into the palace kitchens, she thought. Kitchens meant bustle and rush, people going in and out with goods – she might be able to sneak in unnoticed. Especially if she could get hold of a basket of eggs or vegetables. Dora put one of the aprons on, then slipped out of the yard and down the alley. She joined the crowds streaming towards the main marketplace.

It wasn't hard to exchange a quick and easy wart-removing spell for a basket of eggs, and once Dora had the basket on her arm, she headed for the palace. Picking her way through the mud and manure, Dora reflected on how clean Simon and Cat's world was in comparison to the kingdom. It was just as smelly, though, she thought, with all those cars and buses leaving great trails of stinging fumes behind them. She preferred the smell of dung.

She put her head down as she reached what looked like the scullery yard round the back of the palace, but no one seemed to notice that she wasn't one of the maidservants. Trying not to catch anyone's eye, she followed a girl with a basket of carrots to a storeroom just off the main kitchen. Here, a large, round woman was ticking off goods on a long list.

"Eggs?" said the woman to Dora, as she spotted her. "About time too! Put them there and then get off to Mrs Balsden. She's in a right paddy – needs an extra girl to do the fireplaces."

Dora put down the basket of eggs and then hesitated, wondering who Mrs Balsden was and where she was supposed to go to find her. The woman raised her eyebrows at Dora and gave her a push towards one of the doors. "Go on, don't just stand there. Get on with it!"

Dora slipped through the door into another

room full of noise and bustle. A severe-looking woman in one corner was directing various maidservants around the palace and complaining loudly about their general slowness and inability to understand perfectly clear instructions. *Mrs Balsden*, thought Dora.

"You, girl!" called the woman to Dora. "Stop dawdling and get over here – right now!" But just at that moment one of the maids tripped with a metal bucket full of hot ash, and pandemonium ensued. Dora ducked behind the other servants and eased herself through a small doorway. She closed the door behind her, shutting off the noise of shrieks and angry shouting.

Dora found herself in a narrow corridor that headed into the main palace. She set off along it, trying to look as if she knew what she was doing and where she was going. It wasn't long before she came to a divide, with one branch of the corridor carrying on into dimness, the other heading right, towards a set of stairs. Dora hesitated, and as she stood there a door opened behind her, and a hand clamped onto her shoulder.

"New girl, are you?" came a voice. Dora turned to see a man in a footman's uniform who'd just emerged from a large walk-in cupboard, a pile of linen under one arm.

"Er, yes – I-I'm new," stuttered Dora. "I was looking for –"

"Never mind what you were looking for!" said the man. "I've got a pile of sheets here that needs to go to the Royal Seamstress, and I have no wish to go traipsing off up to the third floor. So you can take them for me." He dumped the pile of sheets in her arms, and then gestured down the right-hand corridor. "Down there, up the stairs to the third floor, second door on your right, go past the turning for the queen's chambers and carry on to the end. All right? Got that?"

Dora nodded, and the man gave her a slight push. "Go on then! You haven't got all day!" He flapped his arms at her and pointed again in the direction of the stairs. Dora bobbed a small curtsey and hurried down the passage, her heart pounding.

She reached the plain spiral staircase at the end of the corridor and started to climb it. She had no idea where to look for Simon, and the palace was like a labyrinth, with servants everywhere. She was bound to get caught if she carried on wandering around looking lost. On the other hand, she now had directions to the queen's chambers. Maybe she should take advantage of that. Go to the queen, get her help. The queen knew about Lord Ravenglass's plans; she'd even met Cat and Simon. And she still had the kingdom's piece of amber – the sky amber.

Dora reached the third floor and stopped to catch her breath. She *would* go to the queen, she decided. It was the most sensible thing to do. Maybe together they could find Simon and get away from the palace before Lord Ravenglass came to seize the last piece of amber.

Chapter Fourteen

Simon was exhausted. Ravenglass was trying to teach him to use Bruni's sword to defend against magic, but it was not going well. It meant mastering the trick of spell-sight, and it had taken Simon all morning to even begin to see the wispy outlines of magic spells. In the end, exasperated by Simon's constant yawning, Ravenglass had sent him to bed for a few hours. It didn't feel as if it had been enough – Simon could barely keep his eyes open – but Ravenglass was insisting on him watching as he conjured the same spell again and again. Simon strained to see the magic as it formed.

"Come on, Simon!" urged Ravenglass. "Concentrate! If you can't see the spells clearly, you can't parry them. And we need to get the sky amber before I go to the Adamantine Sea.

Who knows what kind of powerful magic user has control of the sea amber, eh? I'm not going without all three pieces!"

Simon nodded, and Ravenglass held out his hands again, casting a spell that lifted up the ornate wooden table in the middle of his chambers. Simon squinted at the table, which appeared to be surrounded by a glittering haze. He pressed his lips together, and forced his eyes to focus on the haze. And then, like a picture suddenly coming into focus, he saw it. Around the table was a web of shining strands, with three or four strands leading back to Ravenglass's extended hands.

"I can see it!" he said excitedly. "I can see the spell."

"At last!" breathed Ravenglass, and let the table fall back down to the floor. "Now, Simon, hold up the sword. Like I showed you. Hold it in a defensive position."

Simon took the sword by the hilt and held it in front of his body. As he did so Ravenglass lifted his arms, shaking his velvet sleeves down a little, and prepared to cast a spell. Simon realised that he could see silvery strands gathering in Lord Ravenglass's hands. He watched him tense and then flick his fingers, sending a burst of silver exploding towards Simon. Instinctively, Simon threw the sword up and parried.

As the spell hit his sword there was a deep ringing sound – as if he'd struck the sword against a huge bell – and the silvery magic shattered and fell into little motes of dust that gleamed for a second and then disappeared. Simon felt winded and his arms were aching, but Lord Ravenglass looked pleased. Simon breathed a sigh of relief. He'd done it! He could help get the sky amber.

Lord Ravenglass grinned. "Excellent, Simon. Excellent!" He leaned over and clasped Simon's shoulder. "It's time to go to the queen. With you to defend me, the sky amber is as good as ours. Your father is one step closer to being released."

Dora slipped out into the main third-floor corridor. What had the footman said? Second door on the right? There were several plain wooden doors leading off the corridor, and she pushed the second one open cautiously. The passage beyond was altogether more richly decorated, with dark wooden panelling and a brightly woven rug down the middle of the floor.

Dora tiptoed along the passage till she spotted what must be the turning to the queen's rooms. There was a large set of gilded double doors at the entrance to her chambers, but almost hidden to one side was a simple wooden door. The servants' corridor beyond took her to the back of the queen's antechamber. And there, sitting upright by a tall window, working a delicate piece of lace, was the queen herself.

Queen Igraine looked up as Dora slipped quietly into the room, and gave her a kindly smile. "Ah, my dear," she said. "You must be the new girl. Have you brought the thread I asked for?"

Dora glanced swiftly around. There was no one else in the room. She dumped the linen on a nearby chair and hurried across to the queen.

"Your Majesty, I've come from… the forest agents."

The queen looked puzzled. "Sorry, dear? Did you say you've come to give me a ladle? What would I want a ladle for?"

"No," said Dora, speaking louder. "I'm from the forest *agents*. Lord Ravenglass has managed to get two pieces of amber. He's put a spell on Simon – you met his sister, Cat. I thought…"

Her voice faltered, and she wondered whether coming to the queen had been such a good idea. "I thought maybe you could help."

The queen put her lace down. "Cat and Simon," she said, and then waited, her head tilted, as if listening for an answering echo from the walls around her. After a moment, her face cleared. "I met Cat yesterday!" she said. "Along with Irene."

"Yes!" said Dora, relieved. "They escaped – but her brother, Simon, came back here last night with two bits of amber. Lord Ravenglass put a spell on him – we didn't realise…"

The queen held up her hand for Dora to stop, and reached up to her neck. On a delicate silver chain, attached by woven threads of silver, was the kingdom's piece of amber. It was in the shape of a teardrop, a pale orange stone filled with bubbles of light. She held it and whispered a few words, and Dora could see the glow of the amber brighten till its light escaped between her fingers. It was as if a fragment of a star had fallen to earth and was hanging from the queen's neck. As it glowed, the queen seemed to lose some of the look of faded bewilderment – her eyes cleared and when she turned her gaze on

Dora it was with altogether more authority.

"The amber always helps," she said. "Clears my head a little. Now, where were we?" She stood up and brushed her hands down her dress, smoothing out the dark velvet. "Ravenglass has two pieces of deep amber, is that what you said?"

Dora nodded. The queen pushed some wisps of white hair out of her face and patted the rest absently. "He won't come for the sky amber till he has all the others," she said. "I might get a bit confused occasionally, but I can defend myself from an attack. And my magic's more than a match for him, even if he *has* got two pieces of amber." She hesitated. "But on the other hand, I can't just have him arrested. He has the palace guards more or less under his control now and he's convinced everyone I'm dotty." She raised one eyebrow at Dora. "Maybe it would just be better to leave? See if we can get your friend Simon, and get away to the forest. What do you think?"

But before Dora had a chance to reply, the double doors at the end of the chamber were flung open and Lord Ravenglass strode in with Simon beside him, sword drawn.

Chapter Fifteen

The queen reacted instantly. Holding the sky amber tightly with one hand, she sent a fierce spell hurtling towards Ravenglass. But before it could reach him, Simon stepped forward and the spell broke against his sword with a bell-like tone. Simon staggered slightly, but Lord Ravenglass was completely unharmed. He laughed, a flash of white teeth in his long, handsome face, and held up his hands. From one dangled the orange-brown oval of Cat's amber on its bronze chain, from the other the fire amber glinted bright and golden.

"You can't defeat me, Igraine," he drawled, sounding almost bored. "May as well just hand over that little jewel round your neck right now."

"Not while there's breath in my body," said

the queen, fury in her voice, and she sent another spell storming down at Ravenglass, but again Simon's sword parried it.

"Really?" said Lord Ravenglass with a sigh. "Must I?"

He held the two pieces of amber out in front of him and muttered a few words. Flames seemed to fill the room, and Simon could see the queen almost lifted off her feet by the force of the spell directed at her. But she made a rapid series of hand gestures and the fierce orange light of the flames faded. The queen was still upright, but panting now, her white hair in disarray, her whole body shaking.

Simon readied himself to parry another spell, but the queen was pale, unable for the moment to gather her magic. Ravenglass held out his hand with a satisfied smile on his face. It seemed they had won.

Then Simon noticed a movement behind the queen and a small figure – a servant? – moved out of the shadows and sent a silvery spell straight at Lord Ravenglass. At the same time she shouted, "It's me, Simon! It's Dora!"

Simon blinked. *Dora?* What was *she* doing here?

But now he could see her properly in the light from the window, there was no doubt. Dora had somehow got herself to the kingdom, to the queen's chambers, and she was trying to stop them getting the sky amber.

Simon was so taken aback he forgot to use the sword. He heard a curse behind him, and turned to see Ravenglass flinch as Dora's spell hit – but then the fire amber shone brightly for a moment, and Ravenglass righted himself.

"Simon!" he snarled. "Do your job!" Then he turned to Dora and narrowed his eyes at her. "Meddlesome witch! Out of my way!" He pointed one hand towards Dora and started to mutter the words of a spell.

Simon felt a wave of horror come over him. Ravenglass was about to blast Dora with all the power of the amber. He could see her desperately weaving a barrier spell but he knew it wouldn't hold for more than a few moments. He couldn't let her be hurt!

As Ravenglass's spell hurtled towards Dora, Simon threw himself forward. A deep, ringing note reverberated round the queen's chamber as the spell hit Simon's sword, but his parry was late, and the edge of the spell caught Dora. Her legs folded under her, and she collapsed in a heap on the floor. The queen, too, was in trouble. The sword deflected most of Ravenglass's spell away from Dora, but its power had been sent straight towards the queen, who wasn't expecting it. She was thrown forcibly backwards and, with a sickening crack, she landed heavily on the floor of her chambers.

Simon hurried over and knelt down beside the two figures. Dora's eyes were open, although she was winded. The queen was out cold but still breathing. Simon gave a sigh of relief.

Lord Ravenglass stepped smartly up to the queen. He bent down and unclasped the sky amber from her neck. Then he gave Dora a small, ironic bow and slipped the amber into his coat pocket.

"Your little intervention distracted her nicely," he said. "It was really most convenient." He turned to Simon, one eyebrow raised. "Simon, are you sure you know which side you're on?"

Simon hesitated. There was a fierce pain gathering behind his eyes, making it hard to think. It was pure instinct that had made him throw himself in front of Dora. He didn't want to hurt her. She'd been kind to him, she'd taught him magic. They were *friends*. But on the other hand, Dora was on the side of the Great Forest. That meant she was the enemy.

Simon stood up, and tucked his sword into his belt. "I'm on your side, of course," he said to Lord Ravenglass, trying to ignore the shooting pains in his head. "But it's not her fault she's in league with the forest. She doesn't understand. I – I didn't think we needed to hurt her." He shrugged. "And anyway, it all worked out, didn't it? We've got the amber."

Lord Ravenglass nodded slowly. "We have indeed got the amber. As you say." He flashed a smile at Simon, and then at Dora, lying by the queen. "Although – it really would be simpler to just kill them both, you know. We don't want the forest mounting some ill-considered rescue attempt, trying to stop us before we can get the last piece." He cocked his head to one side, and looked at Simon with a quizzical expression.

Simon caught his breath. He couldn't believe what Ravenglass was suggesting! They needed the amber to rescue Dad, but they had it now.

He didn't want to see Dora hurt – or the queen. Ravenglass was watching him carefully, his eyes cold, and suddenly Simon realised that he was being tested. To see how far he'd be willing to go for his father's release. *Not that far*, thought Simon, but something told him it wouldn't be a good idea to let Ravenglass know that.

"We *could* kill them," he said slowly, "but I don't think Dad would want that. We've got the sky amber now. We could just tie them up, and make sure no one can get in."

Lord Ravenglass held Simon's gaze for a long moment, and then shrugged.

"Of course," he said. "You're right. Your father wouldn't want anyone hurt unnecessarily." He grinned and rubbed his hands together. "We'll bind them," he went on, and conjured a length of strong rope which he handed to Simon. "And gag them. Especially gag them. We don't want anyone muttering any little unbinding spells, do we?"

Simon took the rope, and as he started to bind Dora's wrists, Lord Ravenglass leaned over and murmured in his ear. "We're very close now, Simon. Very close. Don't let me down. *Don't let your father down.*"

Simon shook his head. "Of course not," he said. "Whatever you need me to do."

Lord Ravenglass conjured two gags, and Simon tied them both tightly, first on the queen, and then Dora. Dora tried to catch his eye as he bent over her, but he kept his gaze on the knots, then straightened up.

"It's done," he said to Lord Ravenglass.

"Excellent," said Ravenglass, looking at the tight knots with approval. "I'll tell the palace steward that the queen is having one of her bad days. Sleeping, not to be disturbed." He clapped Simon on the back and smiled. "And now," he said. "I believe I have a ship to catch."

He turned on his heel and left the room. Simon, with a last glance at Dora, followed him.

Chapter Sixteen

Cat dived through the portal to the Adamantine Sea and emerged into a boiling, churning torrent of water. She could barely see Jem's legs kicking in front of her and it took her several moments to work out which direction was up. When she reached the surface, gasping, the hull of the *Merryweather Mermaid* was looming above her, moving rapidly past.

"Jem!" she shouted, and saw his head bob up a short distance away. He looked round, and then swam towards her.

"Cast the spell!" he called. "Make them see us!"

Cat nodded. The Druid had shown her a spell she could use to catch the pirates' attention. She only hoped she could get it to work while also treading water and trying not to swallow half the sea. Reaching her hand out of the waves, she muttered the words, and immediately a spume of water shot upwards and there was a tremendous flash, like lightning. The force of the spell pushed her under water again, and when she spluttered her way to the surface, the *Merryweather Mermaid* looked further away than ever.

"Do you think they've seen us?" said Jem.

"I don't know," said Cat. Her arms were getting tired, and it was hard to stay above the waves. "What do we do if they don't stop?"

"Have to take a portal back – try again," said Jem. "You've got the teaspoon, haven't you?"

Cat groaned. She did have the teaspoon, in one of her pockets, but the thought of doing a portal spell while half drowning – and then having to go through the whole thing all over again – was not a joyful one. She pushed her hair back off her face and squinted at the ship.

"I think… I think it might be turning!" she said. A few moments later she was sure. The ship was slowly altering course and heading back towards them. She could see the huge square sails now, and the mermaid figurehead at the prow, her curly hair streaming back from her face, her fish-tail merging into the stem of the ship. Cat suddenly felt a flash of magic coming from the ship, a kind of magic that reminded her strongly of the power she'd felt in her own piece of deep amber.

"It's on the ship!" she called to Jem. "The sea amber! I can feel it!"

"Well, that's a relief!" said Jem. "At least we haven't got half drowned for nothing!"

The ship was close now. They could see the water foaming and gurgling at her prow as she moved towards them. She was bearing down on them so rapidly that Cat started to wonder if they needed to swim for it before they were run down – but at the last minute the ship turned. Faces appeared above them, peering down from the decks.

"Grab the rope!" called a voice, and a long snaking line curled lazily down from above and smacked into the water just near Jem's head. He took hold of it quickly, and then another line floated down near Cat, who swam across and pulled at it. She looked up to see a young man with mahogany-brown skin and dark curly hair peering down at her.

"There's a loop at the end," he called down. "Put your foot in it and we'll have you up in no time."

Cat found the loop, and the sailors started to heave her aboard. She twisted alarmingly as she rose, scraping and bumping painfully on the wooden planking. At last she reached the rail and slithered over it in an undignified fashion, landing on the deck in a heap of arms and legs. To her annoyance, she could see that Jem, next to her, had managed to stay upright. She scrambled to her feet and came face to face with the young man who'd hauled her aboard. He was wearing a bright red and gold waistcoat, with a gleam of gold visible at his ear in amongst the tangle of brown curls, and he looked as if he was trying not to laugh.

Cat coughed, straightened her clothes, and ran her fingers through her wet hair. "W-we're stowaways," she said defiantly. "We – er – we fell overboard."

The captain of the *Merryweather Mermaid* was surprisingly smartly dressed. He had a trim beard, a clean and well-cut blue coat and highly polished black boots. His only concession to being a swashbuckling pirate was a workmanlike cutlass and a brace of well-oiled pistols attached to his belt. Plus, Cat couldn't help noticing, a rather wicked-looking knife tucked into his boots. Otherwise, he could have been any merchant captain trading out of a respectable sea port.

The hooded eyes that were staring at them out of a deeply tanned and weathered face, however, were as sharp as flint and as grey as a stormy sea. "If you were stowaways," he mused with a frown, "you would have been found before now. And how did you come to suddenly fall off the ship in the middle of nowhere?"

"We were hanging on to the anchor chain," said Jem. "We'd been clinging on to it since you left port – but we couldn't hold on any more. So we fell." He looked round at the pirates surrounding them, his expression a perfect mixture of honesty and eagerness. "Please! We're not spies or anything. We just wanted to join you. My – er – my sister was being forced to marry against her will. And I've always wanted to be a pirate. So she dressed as a boy and cut her hair off and we ran way to join you!"

Cat winced. She had left the details of their story to Jem, but she wished now she'd checked it with him. It all sounded a bit implausible. The men around them, though, seemed willing to believe him. One of them reached over and clapped Jem on the back with a laugh.

"Well, we'll make a pirate of you, young man – no trouble. Once you've spent a few years scrubbing the decks and cleaning out slop buckets!"

The captain gave them both another hard stare, and then shrugged his shoulders. "Very well. I'm Captain Torval. You'll both address me as 'Cap'n' or 'Sir'. You, boy – you'll work your passage, and you'll answer to Mister Trimble." He gestured at a stocky man with a red neckerchief and sweat glistening on his bald head. Trimble grinned at them, revealing about half the number of teeth you'd usually expect, and most of those black.

Jem nodded, and the captain turned to Cat. "You, though. You're a girl. There's no place for a girl on board a ship. You can stay in my cabin till we make port, and then you'll be put ashore."

Jem looked as if he was about to protest, but Cat gave him the slightest shake of the head, and he subsided. She didn't like the idea of getting separated, but if they were going to find the amber, it would be no good for them both to be confined to the crew's quarters. The captain was undoubtedly the master of the stone, and it was more likely to be hidden somewhere in his cabin than anywhere else on board.

She bobbed a curtsey at Captain Torval, trying to appear meek and anxious. It wasn't that hard. He didn't look like a man you'd want to get on the wrong side of. And she was pretty sure that stealing his precious amber jewel would put her firmly on the wrong side of him.

The captain's cabin was dark and smelled of wood, sailcloth and tar. It was full of boxes and drawers and cunningly designed storage cupboards, any one of which could have held a piece of deep amber. Unfortunately, it was also more than half full of the captain himself, sprawled on a bench seat, cleaning his nails with the knife from his boot, and looking Cat up and down with his flinty grey eyes.

"You know, the crew might have accepted your story, but I'm not stupid. I'm pretty sure you appeared out of nowhere – and that means travellers from another world. The boy can stew down there with the crew for now. And you can tell me where you're really from. Tell me now, nice and easy, or tell me later, when I've got a little crosser." He leaned towards her, his eyes holding hers, his knife held steady in his hand. "And that, I don't advise."

Cat swallowed. It was hard to think under the fierce stare of this pirate captain, to say nothing of the strange way her mouth didn't seem to belong to her. Jem had warned her of the way the portal magic twisted your mouth. It allowed you to speak the language of the world you travelled to, but she hadn't been prepared for how strange it would make her feel. The kingdom's language had been close enough to English for the effect to be barely noticeable – but the language of Belhaven made her feel as if she was chewing eels as she spoke.

"I-I'm not from another world," she said. "Really. I don't know what you're talking about. We swam out to the ship in Belhaven. My brother said –" she sniffed, and tried to look as if she was about to cry – "you're good men. You look after the shore people. He said you'd look after us."

The captain frowned. Then he stood up, poked his head out of the cabin, and called across the decks. "Darien! Hey, Darien. Come here!"

He ducked back in, and was soon followed by the lithe young man with the red and gold waistcoat. The captain gestured at Cat.

"She says she's from Belhaven. And they didn't use magic. What do you think?"

The young man turned his thin, watchful face towards her, and Cat swallowed. She could tell that he had magic. Actually, she was fairly certain he had a lot of it. Enough to know, probably, exactly where she'd come from and how. She looked up at him, trying to seem confident and unafraid. But her mind was skipping around frantically, desperate to come up with a plan but finding nothing.

Darien pulled at his ear and hesitated.

"Your name?' he said. He seemed to be listening intently, waiting for her to speak.

"I'm… My name is Catrin Arnold," she said. His eyes widened and she cursed herself. She couldn't think why she'd given him her real name. It probably sounded nothing like the name of someone from Belhaven. But the name she'd agreed with the Druid had gone clean out of her head.

There was a moment's pause, and then the young man turned to Torval and grinned. "She's from Belhaven," he said. "And I think she's telling the truth. She's got no magic. She's no threat to us."

 # Chapter Seventeen

Jem was on his hands and knees with a bucket of seawater nearby, scrubbing at a particularly stubborn stain on the deck, when he felt a touch on his shoulder. It was Cat. Her blonde hair was damp from the sea spray, and her blue eyes were troubled.

"We got away with it," she said. "But only just. That boy with the red waistcoat – Darien. He's got magic. He covered up for me, I'm sure of it. But I have no idea why."

Jem sat up and shrugged. "Well, whatever the reason, let's just find the amber and get out of here. I've decided I definitely don't want to be a pirate. Too much scrubbing. And judging by the rest of the crew, it's pretty hard to keep your teeth at sea. If the scurvy doesn't get you, someone who's drunk too much rum will punch a load of them out."

He sloshed the bucket over the side and stowed the scrubbing brush. "Did you see anything in the captain's cabin?" he said, keeping his voice low.

"No," said Cat. "I had a good look. Then I said I felt ill, needed some fresh air. How about you?"

"No chance to search," said Jem. "Been nose to the deck since you went. Old black-teeth Trimble's a slave-driver. But it's getting near sunset now – and from what the crew say there are celebrations tonight. Rum and music. We should get a chance to do a bit of sneaking around while they're occupied."

Cat leaned over the side of the ship and contemplated the sea. The water was a startling deep blue colour, and where the sun touched it, it glittered silver. *The Adamantine Sea*, she thought. According to the Druid, the seabed was covered in adamantine stones. They gave the sea its colour and its sparkle. It was like sailing a sea of molten sapphire.

"I've tried feeling for the amber," she said. "It's definitely here. But it's as if it's all around us – I can't pin it down to one place. The power of it seems to run though the whole ship."

Jem grimaced. "Maybe it does. After all, they're using it to take the ship across worlds, aren't they?" He leaned a little closer. "I wonder if they'll cross worlds tonight? They raided a merchantman earlier today, they said, so they'll need to make sure they disappear before they get chased down. Maybe when they actually use the amber, you'll be able to work out where it's hidden."

The crew of the *Merryweather Mermaid* certainly knew how to have a celebration. Darkness had fallen swiftly once the sun went down, but the ship was lit up by a multitude of lanterns swinging from the rigging, and the smell of stew and rum was wafting across the decks. There had been a clamouring for music, and Darien had pulled out an old cracked fiddle and was playing wild, strange gypsy music that made the crew stamp their feet and roar.

Cat was sitting on an old salt barrel with Jem, watching the spectacle. She was sending her magic out yet again, trying to feel for the amber. It was here, she was sure of it. She could feel the power of it, nearby. It sang inside her, but the tingle of it in her blood kept getting mixed up with the way Darien's fiddle music was weaving in and out of the rigging, teasing the drunken, stamping sailors and whirling up into the air.

She studied his lean, dark face, the swift movements of his fingertips along the neck of the violin, his arm an extension of the bow dancing across the strings. He knew, she was sure of it. He knew she wasn't from Belhaven. But he'd covered for her. *Why?*

As she watched him, he glanced across, and his mouth turned up ever so slightly at the corners. His whole body was moving with the music, feet tapping, arms and fingers flying, head bent in concentration over the fiddle – but his dark eyes held hers steadily as the tempo started to speed up, and the crew's shouts and stamps grew louder. Cat held her breath as the music grew fiercer and wilder, and the feeling of magic in the air thickened. All at once, she knew where the amber was. She could feel its power, pulling at her. She could almost see it.

She leaned over, and put her mouth close to Jem's ear.

"It's in the prow. The amber. It's somewhere right at the front of the ship."

Jem nodded and together they slipped between the sailors and up to the foredeck. Cat could feel the magic of the amber increasing as she got closer, and as she reached the prow she realised. It was part of the figurehead. It was part of the mermaid herself. She held on to the rail and leaned over the front of the ship.

The mermaid stared out over the Adamantine Sea, her long curly tresses streaming out behind her, her shapely carved arms merging with the timbers of the ship. The bright sparkle of her eyes reflected the moonlight. On one side, her eye was blue – just ordinary painted wood. But on the other, it was a glowing translucent green. Cat knew at once that she was looking at a piece of deep amber, embedded in the wood of the figurehead.

The amber stone was the green of the sea depths and on the surface glints of bright gold swirled and danced like the reflections of sunlight on water. Around it, twists of copper wire in the shape of a shell fixed the stone firmly in the mermaid's carved face.

Cat looked at Jem and nodded. Somehow they would have to prise it out of the figurehead, now, while the pirates were busy with their celebration. Jem pulled out the knife he'd been given for scraping barnacles off the ship's timbers, and prepared to dig into the polished dark wood. But as he did so, the music got louder and suddenly Darien was there, stamping his feet and twirling between them, his bow dancing over the fiddle strings. The pirates around him clapped and shouted, and Jem and Cat were whirled off into the dance, hands pulling them on, voices laughing and calling, and the music rising like sparks of fire into the dark sky.

It was morning before Cat woke. Someone was shaking her, and for a moment she thought she was at home, in bed, and it was Simon… But then she realised she was lying on the deck of a ship, and she could see Jem's long nose and freckled face hovering anxiously above her.

"Cat!" he was saying. "Cat! Worlds above! Wake up!"

"W-what's happening?" she croaked. All around was the noise of shouting sailors, the creak of timbers and the flap of sails being hauled towards the wind. The ship was shuddering, and leaning quite dangerously to one side, she thought.

Cat felt stiff and her throat hurt. Dimly she remembered feasting and music and smoking lanterns swinging from the rigging, lighting up the decks with a yellow glow. She'd danced, she thought, feeling the aches in her limbs. She rubbed her eyes, trying to remember. Had she danced with Darien? She had a memory of the young man handing his fiddle to another sailor and pulling her into a whirling dance all around the ship, while the rest of the crew clapped and stamped their feet. They must have all just collapsed and slept on the deck. But what was going on now? Why all the shouting and running around?

"We're being chased," said Jem, grabbing her arm and hauling her to her feet. "There's a ship – the captain thinks it's from Belhaven, from the merchant's guild. It's armed with canons. And it seems to be gaining on us."

The sun had just risen behind them. As Cat squinted across the glinting sea, she could just make out a ship. It was tiny, no more than a smudge on the horizon.

"It's a long way behind," she said.

One of the sailors turned as he hurried past, and gave her a gap-toothed leer. "She's a fully rigged clipper – three masts, see? She's overhauling us fast. We'll be sunk inside an hour if the captain can't shake her off."

"An hour?" said Cat, startled. "But – Jem! The amber!"

"I know," he said. "Now might be a good moment – while they're all busy."

Cat nodded, and the two of them made their way to the front of the ship. But there, standing right at the prow, was the captain. And he appeared to be arguing rather heatedly with Darien, who had his fiddle and bow in his hands.

"We shifted last night. They can't be from Belhaven," the young man was saying.

Torval grimaced. "I know a Belhaven rig when I see it. That clipper's the *Adventurer*, or I'm a pig farmer from Rode. So we never shifted last night. We're in the Belhaven slice of the Sea and you need to do something about it, quick, before we're overhauled."

Darien pressed his lips together and nodded. He took the fiddle and, tucking it under his chin, lifted his bow. *He's going to play now?* thought Cat, confused. What was going on? But then the music started. It was a slow, haunting melody, the notes not so wild as last night, but pure and clear. They pulled at her, made her feel as if she was being lifted into the air, the drawn-out notes stretching like silvery threads across the wide ocean. And then she felt the magic take hold and realised. He was controlling the amber – using music to connect with it, tap its power. The whole ship was being drawn along the threads of sound into another world – one the Adamantine Sea still touched, but a long way away from Belhaven and the pursuing clipper.

Cat looked across at Darien and saw that he was watching her. As her eyes met his, he nodded ever so slightly. *So it was him*, she thought. He was the heir – not the captain. The amber was his.

Chapter Eighteen

There was a sudden cheer from the sailors on the *Merryweather Mermaid*, and Darien's fiddle-playing stopped with a flourish. Behind them the pursuing clipper had simply vanished. The blue sea stretched out to the horizon, and the sun shone down on a glittering expanse of empty water.

Captain Torval slapped Darien on the back. "Good man," he said. "Once again the *Mermaid* slips their grasp, eh?"

Darien nodded lightly, and then, as the captain busied himself with orders for a new heading and a new trim of the sails, he stepped over to where Cat was standing, and leaned on the rail of the ship next to her.

She turned to him, wondering what to say, whether to tell him that she knew about the amber. After some hesitation, she said, "You have magic."

He nodded.

"But you said I was from Belhaven. You must have known… well…" Her voice trailed off.

He glanced at her sideways, then went back to looking at the water. "I knew you weren't from Skarron," he said. "But if you were free, if you thought you were safe, I guessed I'd have more chance of finding out why you were here. I knew you had something to do with the amber. I could feel its magic in you, too."

He turned and his brown eyes met hers steadily.

Cat hesitated, then nodded. "Yes," she said. "I have – I *had* – another piece of amber. The earth amber."

Darien grinned. "You know, I'd have known you weren't from Belhaven even if it hadn't been for the magic," he said, his eyes dancing. "You're far too pretty to be from the Isle of Skarron."

Cat felt her face grow hot, but before she could answer, Jem sauntered over and leaned casually on the rail beside them. "So," he said, "Darien's the heir, is he?"

Darien gave Jem a calculating look. "The sea

amber came to me from my father," he said. "It belonged to his father, and his father's father – back to my ancestor, King Karon, who was beheaded when the Divided Kingdom was – well, divided. My family have been exiles all that time, hoping we might one day get our kingdom back. Captain Torval and I have been using the amber to stay away from our enemies – to make life a little better for some of the people in the worlds the Sea touches."

He gave a short laugh, and then turned back to Cat, his eyes grave. "It's foolish, but there's a prophecy, in the Divided Kingdom, that the four pieces of amber will come together at a time of great danger to all the worlds. I wondered if that time was now."

Cat took a deep breath. "I think it is," she said. "We… we need the sea amber. We came to try and get it away from here – before it's taken by an enemy of the Great Forest. Will you… Would you come with us? Help us?"

"My family always hoped the amber would help us regain our kingdom," said Darien slowly. Then he shrugged, and grinned at them both. "Myself, I don't much care for kingdoms. The life of an honest pirate suits me just fine. So, if it's time for the amber to serve a more important purpose… Yes, I'll come with you."

Cat felt a wave of relief. They weren't going to have to steal the amber, after all. It was going to be freely given – and even better, the heir who owned it was going to come along and help.

But at that moment, there was a shout from the lookout – and then an answering groan from the crew. The three-masted square rigger had crashed out of nowhere, its black hull now plainly visible, its white sails billowing out, the sea foaming at its prow. Cat felt Jem touching her on the shoulder.

"It's them, isn't it?" he said in a low voice. "Smith and Jones. And they've taken the ship across worlds – so Ravenglass must be with them."

Cat swallowed. She was very much afraid that Jem was right. In the tall black ship, pursuing them, were almost certainly Mr Smith and Mr Jones. And if the ship was following them across worlds then Lord Ravenglass must be on board, with the other pieces of amber.

The tall black clipper was much closer now. Cat could see every detail of the rigging, and the figures of the sailors scurrying about the deck, hauling on ropes and changing the angle of the sails so as to get every last inch of advantage over the *Merryweather Mermaid*. The *Mermaid* herself was flying through the water, heeled over, the sea churning along her sides, spray glittering in the early morning sunlight. Cat squinted into the sun, trying to see if she could see the two crow men or Ravenglass, but they were nowhere to be seen. There was no doubt they were there, though, drawing on the magic of the amber jewels to force the *Adventure* on faster, to guide her immediately across worlds just after the *Mermaid* shifted.

Cat glanced across at Darien. He was playing a fast, wild tune, the notes and tempo constantly changing, the music being whipped away by the wind as the *Mermaid* slipped between worlds as rapidly as his playing could pull her. But however fast they went – the ship heaving over, the ropes straining, the canvas as taut as Darien's bow strings – still the black ship pursued them, gaining on the *Mermaid* with each lurch into a new world.

Cat pulled at Darien's arm. "We've got to go!" she shouted. "There's still time to get to the forest! We have to take the amber before –"

But it was too late. The dark shadow of a bird fell across her and she could see a second shadow weaving between the rigging. With a crack, one of the *Mermaid*'s masts split in two above them and a tangle of sails and ropes came sliding down to the deck. The ship shuddered, and Cat felt a cold breath on the back of her neck.

"So nice to see you again," came a rasping voice from behind her, and she turned to see Mr Jones stretching his thin lips into an icy smile. Just across from him, Mr Smith was lowering his hand and contemplating the mess of rigging and sailcloth with satisfaction. "That should about do it, eh, Mr Jones?" he said.

"Indeed, Mr Smith. Indeed. And now for the amber."

The two dark-suited men started to stalk towards the front of the ship, ignoring the pirates, who were frozen in stark terror. Darien waded across the mess of rope and broken spars, trying to get to the figurehead. Cat saw Jem, almost there too, and Captain Torval taking great strides across the deck, gesturing at the two men in dark suits.

"Hands off my ship!" roared Torval, but Mr Smith barely flicked a finger at him and the pirate captain sank to his knees, gasping for breath. Jem, more circumspect, was trying to creep around behind the windlass, his knife in his hands, but he had hardly got within a few paces of the prow before Mr Jones, with a grin, pointed at the windlass, and it shattered into a thousand specks of dust. Jem looked a little taken aback, and Mr Jones laughed.

"Foolish boy," he said. "Do you really think that you can stop us?"

"The amber will stop you," said Darien, taking a step forward to stand next to Jem. "As long as I control it, you won't be able to take it from the ship."

Mr Smith frowned. "He's right. He's an heir."

The two men stood still for a moment, contemplating the young sailor. Then Mr Jones snapped his fingers. "Nothing else for it. We'll have to call on his lordship."

As he spoke, the *Adventure*, which had been rapidly approaching, came up alongside the *Mermaid*, and its crew started to leap aboard and make fast a number of thick ropes. The two ships came together under full sail with a juddering crash, a groan of ropes and creaking timbers. A gangplank was thrown across, and onto it stepped a tall, elegant figure in a velvet coat.

Shaking out his lace cuffs with a lazy smile, and holding three pieces of amber in one hand, Lord Ravenglass sauntered across the gangplank and onto the foredeck of the *Merryweather Mermaid*. He nodded at Smith and Jones. "The sea amber, please. At once."

The two men gestured at Darien, standing defiant near the prow, holding his fiddle and bow ready. Lord Ravenglass cocked his head towards the young man, and then stretched out his right hand. The three pieces of amber he held swung gently from their chains, their fiery glow intermingling. Darien stood for a moment, sweat beading on his face, and then fell to his knees, as if a great weight was pressing him down.

"You won't be able to cut it from the mermaid," he gasped. "It won't be separated from the figurehead."

Mr Jones laughed, with a sound like bones being shaken in a jar. "As if we care about that," he said.

Mr Smith made a chopping motion with his arm, and the entire figurehead came free of the prow with a splitting groan. As it fell, he reached out with his right hand. The mermaid's head flew through the air towards him and he tucked it under his arm as if it weighed no more than a piece of bread.

Lord Ravenglass was smiling now, and turning towards Darien and Jem. Cat started to move quietly forward, pulling Albert's forest leaf out of her pocket as she crept across the mess of broken spars and ropes. Ravenglass stretched out his hand and contemplated the amber jewels swinging in front of him.

"A most satisfactory conclusion," he said. "But now, I think, just to tie up loose ends…"

He started to mutter a few words and Cat watched in horror as the amber pieces in his hand began to glow. She threw herself towards Jem and Darien, the forest leaf held tightly in her hand. She reached them just as Lord Ravenglass finished speaking and, as his magic hit, she gabbled the word that would activate the leaf and closed her eyes.

Chapter Nineteen

Simon lay on the four-poster bed in his chambers, watching his servant pottering about tidying the room. It was dark outside, and the only light was from a few candles and the glow of the fire. It had been a long day. Lord Ravenglass had left him in charge of a huge list of items they needed for the remaking of the crown. Gradually they had been gathered up and put carefully into wooden crates in a small room just off the palace courtyard. It had taken hours to get all the items checked off and packed.

Simon's head was pounding. It felt as if an entire army was marching up and down inside it, feet tramping rhythmically on the inside of his skull. His headache had started in the queen's chambers, and it hadn't improved through all the sorting and packing of precious metals, spell ingredients and strange bits of equipment. Questions had kept repeating themselves in Simon's mind. *Why had Ravenglass wanted to kill Dora and the queen? Was he to be trusted?* But if not, then why was he helping Dad? All afternoon, images had kept flashing through Simon's head – Lord Ravenglass with his bright white smile; the two dark crow men, Smith and Jones; the round, cheerful face of Albert Jemmet; the crooked grin of the Druid... And the gaunt, pale face of his father, trapped in the ice and snow.

When he thought about the ice cave, Simon felt a fierce stabbing pain in his head. An image flashed into his mind of the hungry, twisted smile on his father's face when he'd seen the pieces of amber – the intensity of his pale eyes. Simon's stomach clenched. He *wanted* the figure in the ice to be Dad – wanted so much to believe that he was alive, that he could be saved. But when he thought of that expression a cold fear seemed to grip the back of his neck and sweep through his whole body.

It isn't Dad, he thought, and it was as if he suddenly put down a heavy weight he'd been carrying around all day. The man in the icy prison wasn't Gwyn Arnold. Simon had been tricked. Ravenglass had put another spell on him. The man in the ice was Lukos.

Lukos.

Simon pulled the heavy curtain of his bed across so the servant couldn't see him, and hugged his knees. Tears trickled down his face. He'd come all this way to rescue his dad, brought the amber jewels, helped fight the queen – but Gwyn was dead. He was *dead*. Simon shut his eyes and clenched his fists as he thought of the man who had tricked him. Lord Ravenglass.

Ravenglass was very close now to winning – to releasing the Lord of Wolves. And the worst of it was that Simon had helped. He'd brought two pieces of deep amber. He'd helped Lord Ravenglass get the third. And now Ravenglass was about to return with the last piece.

There was a faint chirruping sound near Simon, and he turned to see the little furry creature, Frizzle, hopping across his pillow. Simon put out his hand and ruffled Frizzle's feathers, and the little creature purred and nibbled Simon's fingers gently. Simon wiped his eyes with the back of his hand, then tickled Frizzle under the chin. *I need to get out of here*, he thought. *I need to get to the queen's chambers.*

He pulled back the curtains and started to get out of bed. But then he saw the servant, sitting in a chair by the door, his eyes watchful.

"Can I help you, my lord?" he said, half rising.

Simon shook his head, and retreated. Ravenglass must have left orders to keep an eye on him. He couldn't risk rousing suspicion. He would just have to wait till the servant fell asleep.

When Simon finally managed to creep to the queen's chambers, it was hours past midnight. Simon pushed the door open quietly and peered inside.

The pale light of dawn shone through the narrow window by the queen's bed. Dora and Queen Igraine were huddled together on the floor, two deep shadows, immobile, their breathing regular. As Simon tiptoed up to them, Dora stirred and opened her eyes.

"Dora!" he whispered. "I'm so sorry!"

He pulled his sword from his belt, and carefully cut the ropes around her wrists and ankles. Gently, he used the very tip of the sword to slice away the gag that was cutting into her mouth, and she pulled it away with relief.

"Simon!" she said. "You broke the spell!"

"In the end," he said, with a grimace, as he turned to the queen and started freeing her from her bonds. "But not till this evening. And then I couldn't get away – Ravenglass left a servant to guard me. I had to wait till he fell asleep."

The queen coughed and wheezed slightly. Dora put her arms round Igraine's shoulders and Simon leaned over to help. Between them they got the queen to a sitting position, propped up against her bed. She pushed some stray bits of white hair out of her face and gave Simon a vague smile.

"So nice of you to visit," she said in a hoarse voice. "I'll order tea directly. Just as soon as I – well…"

Her hand drifted to her neck, and she felt around for the jewel that was no longer there. She turned to Dora and seemed to make a huge effort to pull herself together. "Did my blasted nephew – did he *take my amber?*"

Dora nodded. "He's got three now," she said

loudly. "He's close to being able to remake the crown."

"The amber crown," said the queen. Her expression was bleak. "The foolish boy."

"So, what are we going to do?" said Simon, trying to keep his voice steady. "What's happening back home?"

"Cat and Jem were going to the Adamantine Sea when I left," Dora said. "They were trying to get the sea amber."

"I think Ravenglass has gone there too," said Simon. "He said he had a ship to catch."

Dora turned pale. "They won't be expecting him," she said. "They knew Smith and Jones would be a danger, but they won't be prepared for Lord Ravenglass. Not with three pieces of amber."

Simon felt cold. Cat was there, somewhere on the Adamantine Sea. Even if she and Jem had managed to find the sea amber, Ravenglass would be close behind. Quite possibly he'd already caught up with them.

"But that's not all," said Dora, sitting up urgently. "Your mum and Albert left yesterday morning to come to the kingdom." She glanced out of the window, at the gradually lightening sky. "They should have been here ages ago. I think they must have got caught."

"Mum?" said Simon. "She's *here*?" He slumped against the bed. Cat was in danger – and Mum was here, quite possibly in the palace dungeons right now. And it was *his fault*. He'd come here, he'd brought Ravenglass the fire amber and the earth amber. He'd helped him get the sky amber from the queen.

He groaned.

"So, do we try and get after Lord Ravenglass? Maybe – with the sword – we could stop him?"

"I think we need to leave," said Dora. "See if we can find out what's happened to Albert and your mum. We can't help Cat and Jem, and we can't stay here – Ravenglass might be back at any minute."

Simon nodded and stood up. He tucked the sword back onto his belt and held his hand out to the queen. "You're right," he said to Dora. "Let's get out of here."

But before any of them could move there was a resounding crash from the queen's window. An ornate vase, which had been sitting on a small shelf nearby, was now on the floor, knocked flying by a brawny arm in a blue sleeve. Attached to the arm, and hauling himself over the window ledge with a certain amount of puffing and blowing, was the stocky figure of Albert Jemmet.

"Give us a hand, won't you?" he called, seeing them all staring at him in consternation. "I think I might be stuck."

Chapter Twenty

Albert squeezed his way through the narrow window and pulled himself upright with help from Dora and Simon. He glanced round the room, at the ropes on the floor and the queen sitting looking rather dishevelled by the bed.

"Ah," he said. "Things not going so well, then." He bowed to the queen, and his shrewd blue eyes took in the lack of a jewel at her neck. "And the sky amber gone."

The queen put her hand up to her throat. "Ravenglass took it," she said. "The boy's gone mad. Remaking the crown..." She sighed. "I should have left before, when Irene told me. I could have had the amber safe in the forest." A tear trickled down her check, and Dora gave her a comforting pat on the shoulder.

"Well, it's a pity you didn't and that's a fact," said Albert. "But at least you're all safe – and I'm glad to see you here, Simon. Broke the spell, did you?"

Simon nodded.

"Good lad," said Albert with satisfaction. "Thought you might."

"Where's Mum?" said Simon, moving to the window and peering down. There was a large drop to the battlements below. It looked as if Albert had climbed up a rather tangled growth of ivy. But there was no sign of anyone following him.

"We got caught," said Albert. "Ravenglass had had all the forest agents arrested. The house we took a portal to was being watched. He wasn't taking any chances – must have guessed there'd be a rescue attempt. They chucked us in a spell-proof dungeon, so it took forever to escape. Florence stayed to get the other forest agents out. I said I'd get the queen and you, Simon – try and make sure we got one bit of amber safe, at least." He looked round at them all. "Seems I'm too late for that. But I'm here now, so we can get you lot back at least. And the others are all safe in Wemworthy."

"No they're not," said Dora, her expression anguished. "Cat and Jem went to the Adamantine Sea. And Ravenglass has gone after them."

Albert looked startled. "They went to the Sea? And Ravenglass has gone there too?"

"With all three pieces of amber," said Simon heavily. "He left hours ago. Said he was going to a ship – that he'd be back shortly with the last piece."

Albert made a face. "We'll have to hope they have the sense to get out of his way," he said. "Or he'll have it off them, no messing. They couldn't stand against three pieces of amber."

Dora felt as if great bands of iron were tightening around her chest till she could hardly breathe. She knew as well as she knew her own name that Jem would fling himself between Lord Ravenglass and the sea amber without any hesitation. He was going to be blasted with the same spell that had come hurtling towards her only yesterday. But without Simon to deflect it.

She looked across at Simon. His face was almost grey, his eyes staring at her. A terrible silence fell in the room as all of them thought about what might be happening right then on the ship in the Adamantine Sea.

Queen Igraine shook her head. "Well, it's no use worrying about it," she said with a sigh. "We're not going to last much longer than them, anyway. Ravenglass will soon have all four pieces. So we've lost."

"No," said Albert quickly. "There's still a chance to stop him. The forest has always known he might succeed in getting all four pieces. But there's one thing he doesn't know – and won't be prepared for. The amber pieces still have an affinity for the previous heirs." He leaned down towards the queen. "If we can get you to the remaking," he said loudly, "you could stop him using the full power of the sky amber."

The queen frowned. "Stop him using the full power…?" she repeated slowly. After a moment's thought, she nodded, and sat up straighter, her eyes brightening "You're right! There's a chance that would work."

Albert turned to the others. "Ravenglass has got control of the pieces of amber at the moment. But he only took control recently, and soon he'll be trying to hold all four. His power over them will be weak. Each piece is still connected to its previous owner. The longer they owned it, and the stronger their magic, the better that connection will be."

"So, the queen could influence the amber that was hers?" said Dora. "She could take its power back again?"

"Not while he's directly wielding it," said Albert. "But if she was present at the making she might be able to stop the amber binding completely to the Old Iron of the crown. And then we'd have a chance to defeat him."

"And if all else failed," said the queen brightly, "there's the sword."

"The sword?" said Simon.

"Didn't you know?" said Queen Igraine, looking round at them. "Bruni used his sword to break the crown last time. If Ravenglass does manage to remake the crown, then that sword – the one you've got there – is the only thing that can destroy it."

There was a moment's silence.

"But then – we have to know exactly where he's going to do the magic," said Simon. He felt as if he could hardly breathe.

Albert looked at him steadily. "We do," he said. "The forest has been trying to find out what they can. They're pretty sure it will be somewhere in your world. It's where it all happened last time, and it's a rich source of Old Iron. But they can't find the exact spot. Lou was going to do some digging on the internet, see if he could see signs of anything unusual brewing. But we can't guarantee we'll find it in time."

Simon hesitated. He felt as if he was teetering on the edge of a precipice. Now he was about to step off into nothing. But the words were out of his mouth before he had a chance to feel afraid.

"I'll be able to tell you," he said. "If I stay with Ravenglass, I'll be with them when they do the magic. If you can give me a way of letting you know – some kind of spell – then I could lead you to them."

"But Simon!" said Dora. "It's horribly dangerous. What if he realises you've broken his spell? What if he puts another one on you? Isn't it safer for you to come back with us – bring the sword? Maybe the Druid will be able to find out where the crown will be made?"

Simon shook his head. "He might not be able to do it in time," he said stubbornly. "Whereas I'll *know*. And it might be dangerous, but it's going to be pretty dangerous being anywhere at all. He's planning to destroy the worlds, Dora! That's *everywhere*! Besides, I have to do something. It's my fault he got all the pieces of amber in the first place."

"It is *not* your fault," said Dora fiercely. "He was just too clever for us – all of us. You don't have to do this!"

"I'm sorry," said Albert. "But I think Simon's right. It's our best chance. And if he's going to do it, he needs to go soon. Ravenglass may be back at any moment. And he'll expect Simon to be in his chambers."

"I'll need a way to let you know where I am," said Simon, trying to sound matter of fact. "When… when they start the making."

Albert felt in his overall pocket, and then his face fell. "Damn," he said. "I was going to give you my forest leaf, but I gave it to Lou. The queen should have one."

He turned to Queen Igraine. "Your forest leaf," he said. "We need to give it to Simon."

The queen nodded, and reached into a hidden fold of her dress. She pulled out a small golden leaf. "Every monarch of the kingdom is given one," she said as she handed it to Simon. "A sign of the alliance between the kingdom and the forest." She patted Simon on the back and smiled encouragingly. "Keep it well hidden."

"What does it do?" said Simon.

"You just need to tear it in half, when you're sure you're in the right place," said Albert. "The forest will know it's been torn – and exactly where you are. We'll be there as fast as we can. And if you think Ravenglass suspects you, if there's any danger – use it to get to the forest. It's a simple spell word, that's all. Take you there as quick as winking."

He leaned over and whispered the word in Simon's ear. Simon nodded, and tucked the leaf into his hoody pocket. Dora threw herself at Simon and gave him a fierce hug. She wanted to say something encouraging, or give him some advice, but she found she couldn't speak. Simon hugged her back and took a deep breath.

"I'd better get back to my rooms," he said. "Wait for Ravenglass."

"Good lad," said Albert, clapping a hand on Simon's shoulder. "You'd have made your father proud. I'll get these two safely down to your mum

– said I'd meet her in the stables in half an hour. Then I'll get everyone back to Wemworthy. We'll be waiting for your signal."

Simon nodded and tried to give them all a grin, but he wasn't sure he'd succeeded. He turned abruptly and walked out of the room. Nodding to a couple of sleepy servants just starting to bustle around the corridors, he set off to his own rooms, trying to control a slight twitch in the corner of one eye, and a trembling in his hands. *It's going to be all right*, he told himself. *It's going to be all right.*

Chapter Twenty-one

Inanna sat on the garden bench in the weak morning sunlight and thought about Ur-Akkad. She'd been so eager to leave, to go on an adventure in a strange world, to get away from the horrible Chief Ensi, Ra-Kaleel. But it was cold here, and boring, and she missed the warm bright colours of her home. For the first time, she found herself wondering what she would do when – if – they defeated Lord Ravenglass. The magic users in the Akkadian Empire would have been released – the fire amber that kept them trapped and drained their magic was no longer there. If she went back, she'd be free to use her magic to help the city. She'd no longer be in danger of being locked up because of it.

"Sir Bedwyr?" she called. The knight was

pottering about the garden, snipping off bits of plants here and there. Inanna was pretty sure some of them were ones Great-Aunt Irene had pointed out as her prized camellias. She was also pretty sure Sir Bedwyr knew exactly what he was doing.

"Your Highness?" said Sir Bedwyr, turning to her with a flourish of his secateurs.

Inanna smiled. He really was very handsome, she thought. Much more so than Jem, who had a rather long, freckled face. Sir Bedwyr had perfect tanned skin and startling blue eyes.

"I was wondering," she said, "what you were planning to do, when this is all over."

The knight came over and sat down next to her on the bench. "I don't know," he said. "I *was* on a quest. For a dragon."

"We have dragons in Akkadia," said Inanna.

Sir Bedwyr turned to her, interested. "Big ones?" he said. "Wild ones?"

She nodded. "There are red dragons in the palace labyrinth," she said. "They're pretty dangerous, but they're not exactly wild. But out in the desert there are hundreds. All sorts of varieties."

Sir Bedwyr's blue eyes took on a faraway

expression. "All my life," he said, "I've dreamed of hunting wild dragons. We have a dragon near the castle – the Druid brought it. But no one's allowed to hunt it. It's a kind of mascot."

"I'm pretty sure you'd be a hero in Akkad if you were prepared to hunt a few dragons," said Inanna. "The farmers hate them. Always destroying their crops. To say nothing of eating stray children."

She tilted her head, regarding him through her long eyelashes. "I could make you a knight of Akkad," she said. "You could help me restore my kingdom. And you would be able to hunt as many dragons as you like."

Sir Bedwyr regarded her quizzically for a few moments, and then he grinned. He got down on one knee, and took out his sword. "I pledge my fealty to you, most high princess," he said. "I'll aid you in Akkad, and you will point me in the direction of the wild dragons."

"It's a deal," said Inanna, and giggled at the knight's earnest expression.

There was a commotion behind them, and they turned to see Dora emerging into the garden, while behind her the kitchen appeared to be in uproar, with loud voices and bangs and the sound of breaking crockery.

"Dora!" cried Inanna, and ran to give her a hug. "Did you find Simon? Is that Florence I can hear?"

Dora winced as another crash resounded from the kitchen. "Yes, and yes," she said. "We left Simon behind – he's going to try and let us know where the crown will be remade. But Florence isn't very happy about it. Or about Cat having gone to the Adamantine Sea. And as far as she's concerned, it's all the Druid's fault."

It was a good half-hour before Dora, Inanna and Sir Bedwyr dared to creep back into the kitchen. By then it felt strangely silent. Florence was sitting at the table with her head in her hands, and the Druid was standing awkwardly by the sink, fiddling with mugs. Great-Aunt Irene was hovering, ghostly pale, peering out of the back window, and Queen Igraine had fallen asleep in the armchair in the corner. She was snoring gently.

Dora leaned against the cupboards by the Druid.

"Where's Albert?" she said.

"He went to the forest," he said. "To wait for news. He'll come back here as soon as they know anything."

"He said you were going to try looking on the – um – internet thing," said Dora. "Did you find anything?"

The Druid made a face. "Some." He bit the side of his thumb absently, watching the back of Florence's head. "It's odd. There are signs of something going on. I'm sure it's going to be here, in this country. There are ripples... But they don't seem to lead anywhere, or make sense."

He pulled a small, flat box from his pocket and pressed the side. The box lit up, and the Druid's fingers started to dance across its top surface. Dora watched as shapes and pictures moved and changed in response to the Druid's hand movements. *It's like a kind of magic*, she thought. *An electric magic.*

The Druid's fingers stopped moving, and he stabbed at the flat surface.

"You see!" he said, his voice frustrated. "As soon as it seems like I've got a lead, it gets buried in a whole bunch of old stuff. There's plenty here about the World Tree, the Iron Crown, amber and magical swords – but so much of it is myth. Bits of fairy tales, legends and stories – echoes from the last time. From the first time the crown was made. I can't seem to separate out anything that relates to the present. And here's another one! Mysterious lights near an old archaeological dig – but it's from thirty years ago!"

Dora leaned over and peered at the picture on the box. It was grainy, black and white, with bits of writing underneath. She could just make out part of an old stone wall, some trenches, and a man pointing towards a faint glow in the background. The writing was from something called the *Lancashire Guardian*, and it appeared to be about a Roman fort being dug up at… Dora caught her breath, and her heart missed a beat. She tugged at the Druid's arm.

"Did you see where it was?" she said. "Ravenglass! It was in a place called *Ravenglass*!"

The Druid shook his head. "I know. But that place has existed for centuries. Since the Romans. It's got nothing to do with *our* Ravenglass. Just a coincidence."

At that moment, Great-Aunt Irene gave a sudden yelp. They turned to see a portal opening in the middle of the kitchen. Walking out of the mist, holding the silver teaspoon triumphantly in her hand, was Cat. Tumbling after her, with a big grin on his face, was Jem. Dora leapt towards them, as a young man with a bright waistcoat emerged and finally Albert stumbled out of the portal. The kitchen was suddenly very full indeed, with shouts, hugs, laughter and explanations and the busy production of steaming mugs of tea with more than the usual complement of sugar.

"We found ourselves in the forest," said Cat, beaming at them all, Florence's arms wrapped tightly round her. "I managed to get everyone away with the leaf. And then Caractacus found us and we were explaining everything to him and the other forest agents when Albert suddenly appeared! He said we should bring Darien back with us." She gestured at the young man with the red waistcoat.

Dora looked at the lean, dark youth who'd arrived with the others. He was standing quietly near Cat, a fiddle strapped to his back, looking at them all with interest. He seemed unfazed by the new world he found himself in, and all the strange people squashed in around him in the small kitchen. As Cat told everyone the story of their adventures on the *Merryweather Mermaid*, with Jem interrupting and contradicting her, Darien watched the Druid, and Albert, and occasionally glanced at Dora herself. *He's intrigued by the people with magic*, she thought. He had quite a lot of it himself, from what she could tell, but it felt untamed, wild, slightly different. He caught Dora staring at him and smiled. It was a warm, infectious smile, with a hint of laughter in it. Dora hesitated, and then grinned back.

"So," said Albert eventually, putting down his mug of tea with a sigh of satisfaction. "We've got four heirs. And Caractacus will come and tell us as soon as Simon tears the leaf. We've got more than a chance now of stopping Ravenglass."

Florence pulled Cat tighter towards her. "You don't need all four heirs," she said quickly. "You said before you could do it with just the queen. Cat and the others could stay here, out of harm's way."

"*Mum!*" said Cat in outrage, pushing herself out of Florence's arms. "I'm not *staying*! The more of us are there, the better chance we have. And besides, Simon will be there. Everyone should be together…" She hesitated. "In case it doesn't work out. In case we fail."

Florence closed her eyes, and then nodded. She took Cat's hand and squeezed it. "You're right. We'll all go. All or nothing." She laughed, slightly hysterically. "What a bunch," she said, gesturing round the table. "A couple of old ladies, one of them dead already – sorry, Irene, but it's true. A washed-up computer games developer, a few kids, and an odd-job man. All setting off to save the worlds!"

Albert spread his hands out and grinned. "So be it," he said. "But how I see it is, we've got a number of very powerful magic users, some of them heirs of King Bruni, some of them holders of the deep amber." He nodded at Cat, and swept his arm around the table at the others. "And we've got a number of accomplished swordsmen." He bowed to Sir Bedwyr, who raised his sword in salute. "I can't think of a better group of people to have at my back at the end of the worlds."

Chapter Twenty-two

The portal Lord Ravenglass had conjured in the courtyard of the palace was large and solid-looking. Servants hovered, ready to transport the gathered boxes of equipment, and Smith and Jones stood quietly next to them, their dark, watchful eyes on Simon. Lord Ravenglass put his hand on Simon's shoulder, and gestured at the portal. Together they stepped through the white mist.

Immediately, Simon knew he was in his own world. After the kingdom, with its tingling feel of magic everywhere, it was like a blast of cold, fresh wind. And there was plenty of actual cold, fresh wind as well, he realised, as his hair was whipped away from his face and a spatter of fat raindrops blew into his eyes.

"Urgh," said Lord Ravenglass, shaking his

head and pulling his cloak more closely around his velvet jacket. "Blasted country. It's always raining."

They were standing on a flat beach, a mixture of sand, mud and shingle, with grassy tufts at their back and a brownish estuary stretching out for miles in front of them. The other bank, low and flat, was just visible through the drizzle. Simon didn't recognise the place, but the screech of gulls wheeling overhead was a comfortingly familiar sound, and he could sense the sea, just out of sight.

Servants started to emerge from the portal, dragging the heavy boxes. Mr Smith was directing them to pile the boxes up on the sand and then sending them, one by one, back through the misty doorway, while Mr Jones stood by, watching, his eyes like stones. Lord Ravenglass grinned as he saw Simon looking at the growing pile of equipment and then at the few people remaining.

"Worried about having to carry it all, Simon?" he said, rubbing his hands and stamping his feet to keep warm. "Not a problem, dear boy, I assure you. Once we've seen this lot off –" he gestured at the servants – "we'll shift again, and then there'll be *plenty* of helpers for this little collection."

Simon nodded, and fingered the leaf in his pocket. Obviously they weren't at the right place yet, then. He'd have to hang on till he was absolutely sure. Until he'd *seen* Lukos. He shivered.

"Cold, eh?" said Ravenglass sympathetically. "I know – dreadful country. Mr Smith – a cloak, for Lord Simon!"

Mr Smith bowed and then gestured at the nearest servant, who brought Simon a large velvet cloak and then followed the last of the men back into the portal. It closed with a faint pop, leaving only Simon, Ravenglass and the two crow men standing on the beach.

Simon pulled the cloak around himself and tried to ignore the wet drips finding their way down the back of his neck as he watched Lord Ravenglass build a shimmering, silvery spell wall around the four of them and the pile of equipment. Then, standing in the middle, he took an object out of a nearby box. Simon squinted at it. It looked like a short sword – heavy, workmanlike, with a broad blade tapering to a point. He frowned. He'd seen a sword like that before, he was sure of it. In a museum somewhere – or had Mum showed it to him? Just as Lord Ravenglass started muttering the words of the spell, Simon remembered where he'd seen something similar. It was on a school visit to the Roman Museum in Bath. It was a Roman soldier's sword. Was Ravenglass taking them to a museum?

As Lord Ravenglass's spell took hold, Simon felt as if his stomach had been plucked out of his body and hurled into the air. Everything around him was moving – whirling round – colours bleeding into each other, shapes metamorphosing into other shapes. Mr Smith was clutching one of the boxes, looking as if he might be sick. Ravenglass was gritting his teeth and continuing to intone the words of the spell, and the sword was glowing. It was a bright, hard, silver centre around which everything was revolving.

Finally, just as Simon thought he might come apart and be scattered in pieces across several worlds, the whirling stopped. Their surroundings gradually became clearer, and Simon found himself looking at almost exactly the same landscape he'd been staring at a few moments earlier. It was no longer raining and Simon could see further across the estuary, to the shadow of land the other side. The water in between gleamed gold in the last rays of the setting sun, and the gulls were still wheeling, their melancholy cries echoing across the river.

"H-have we – D-did we –?" he stuttered.

"Shift?' said Lord Ravenglass, his face rather pale, his breathing a little ragged. "Certainly we shifted." He bent over, taking deep breaths. "Forgive me, Simon. It's a rather complex spell. Takes it out of you."

There was a sudden shout from behind them, and Simon turned to see a number of men approaching them along the sand. The leader had his arm up in some kind of salute, and the men behind him appeared to be marching in perfect formation across the sand. Simon blinked.

They were – they had to be – Roman soldiers. But they were quite unlike any soldiers he had seen in pictures, or dressed up for re-enactments. As they came closer he could see that they were swarthy, dark, stocky men with lumpy packs and dirty clothing. Their helmets were dull with mud and dented from use, and the faces beneath them looked similarly grubby and dented. Rather than sandals, the soldiers had sturdy boots and woollen leggings, and most were wearing a kind of poncho wrapped round them for warmth. All of them, however, had their right hands resting firmly on the hilts of sturdy, straight swords attached to wide leather belts.

They were too disciplined to be actors, Simon thought, too lean and battle-stained. These were proper soldiers. Real Romans. Ravenglass had taken them into the *past*.

The troop halted a few metres away, and their leader saluted Lord Ravenglass again.

"Hail, Ravenglass!" he said, and Simon frowned, confused. If he was Roman, shouldn't he be speaking Latin? But then he remembered Jem telling them about being able to understand Akkadian, and he realised that it was the portal magic. He *was* speaking Latin – and Simon could understand it! For a few moments he forgot why they were there, what was at stake, and was caught up in the simple excitement of being in the past. In Roman times. Able to understand Latin.

"I need these boxes transported to the fort," Ravenglass was saying, indicating the pile of equipment on the beach. "Take them down to the cavern. And I want Gaius Quintus. And the best blacksmith you have in Glannaventa." He clapped his hands together. "At once!" he said, and the soldier stood to attention and saluted smartly.

Ravenglass turned to Simon with a smile. "We'll leave them to build the forge," he said. "Smith and Jones can supervise. We'll get warm, and get some dry clothes. And I believe a case of excellent wine should have arrived yesterday from Aquitania."

Simon followed him along the hard sand. Gradually he realised that they were walking alongside the outer wall of a fort – a high wall built of small, tightly packed stones looming above the edge of the estuary. As the wall started to curve inland away from the water, Simon could see more soldiers, as well as local villagers, scattered along a cobbled road leading away from the fort. It wasn't long before they reached the main gates, flanked by two imposing towers. The guards, leaning on their tall rectangular shields and looking bored, waved Ravenglass through the gate and he and Simon walked on up a long straight street, past wooden barracks, to a large square. Here the buildings were stone, impressively large, with elegant columns and covered walkways. Ravenglass leaned over and murmured in Simon's ear: "The Praetorium. From which building the fort commander oversees all the people and soldiers in this corner of the most glorious Roman Empire. From which he has control of the most modern, efficient and well-disciplined army to grace these shores until the Norman Conquest." He smirked. "Luckily," he said, with a wink at Simon, "the current fort commander is, in fact, myself."

Simon smiled back, and followed him into the imposing building. They were here, then. In the place where the crown would be forged. As Lord Ravenglass turned his back, Simon put his hands in his hoody pocket and carefully tore the golden forest leaf. He felt a tingle in his hand as the leaf sent its signal to the Great Tree. Now he would just have to wait, he thought. Wait and hope that the others got here in time.

Chapter Twenty-three

Without knowing exactly where the crown would be remade, it was hard to make concrete plans, but Albert insisted that everyone was kept busy and alert. Inanna, particularly, needed more practise to control her magic, and she took herself off to the garden with Great-Aunt Irene and Sir Bedwyr, who agreed to stand by with the garden hose to prevent any major scorching of the shrubbery.

Jem was eager to know more about the internet, so Cat showed him how to use Google and he was soon lost in a maze of leads, following links from Baltic amber to Viking legends. Dora watched the back of his head, bent over next to Cat's as she showed him how to flip back and forth between one picture and another on the computer screen. They were laughing, as an image of a large piece of amber with some kind of creature embedded in it was instantly replaced by one of a rather startled kitten hanging upside-down from a ceiling fan. Dora rolled her eyes and went to help Florence, who was gathering up as many pieces of protective leather armour, daggers, coats and swords as she could find in Great-Aunt Irene's cellar.

"Albert's got an amazing number of swords hidden away down here," she said, looking up as Dora came in. "I had no idea! Enough to equip a small army!"

"Hobby of mine," said Albert cheerfully, unearthing another long wooden box from the corner. "Your aunt never minded me stowing them here. And chances are we'll have to do at least a bit of fighting to get to Ravenglass, so it's lucky I did."

He pulled out a plain, workmanlike sword from the box and held it out, balanced horizontally on his hand. "One of my best," he said, and then took it by the hilt and ran his thumb along the blade.

"You made it?" said Darien, who had joined them.

"Like I said, hobby of mine," said Albert. "Are you any good with a sword?"

Darien held his hand out and took the blade. He gave it a few experimental swishes. When he handed it back, he looked distinctly impressed. "That's a good sword. Well balanced. And yes, I can use a blade. My family never quite gave up on the idea that one day we'd get our kingdom back. Can't have a prince who can't use a sword." He smiled, and his eyes gleamed. "Can't have a pirate who can't use a sword, for that matter."

"Did someone mention swords?" said Jem, coming down the cellar stairs behind Dora. He grinned at her and pushed his red hair back cheerfully. "Can't get the hang of that internet thing," he said. "Too much nonsense to wade through to find anything that makes any sense."

Albert handed him a short blade, and Jem made a few cutting motions with it and nodded. "This'll do," he said, and Florence gave him a thick leather jerkin that looked about the right size.

"Put it on under your jumper," she said. "And the swords are going to have to be strapped to people's backs, under coats. We can't afford to be stopped by the police wherever we end up."

Dora helped Jem get the sword strapped in place, and then it was Sir Bedwyr's turn to be called down and dressed in more inconspicuous clothing, with his sword tucked neatly away under a dark trench coat that used to belong to the Druid. Inanna, who had come down after him, pulled at the lapels and adjusted the collar, then stood back critically to admire his new look.

"Very handsome!" she declared, and Sir Bedwyr blushed.

Dora leaned over to Jem. "I think you've lost your chance of marrying a princess," she said mischievously, keeping her voice low.

Jem looked horrified. "Marry Inanna?" he hissed. "Whatever gave you the idea that I wanted to *marry* her?"

"Well, you know… I thought you wanted to rescue princesses and all that…"

"Rescue," said Jem loftily. "*Rescue* princesses is what I wanted to do. Not marry them. I'm never going to marry anyone. But if I did decide to marry someone, I know who it would be."

Dora looked up at his familiar freckled face and felt a rather strange hollow feeling start to build inside her stomach. She followed the direction of his gaze to where Cat was choosing a short knife to tuck into her belt, and a heavy coat to cover it.

"She's very pretty," she whispered, her voice oddly choked.

Jem turned to her in surprise. "Who's very pretty?" he said.

"Cat."

He gazed at her in consternation. "You think… Hang on – *Cat*? Dora – you are such an idiot. She's soft on that pirate, anyway."

Dora looked at Darien, whirling two of Albert's swords around his head, one in each hand, while Cat ducked, laughing. She thought Jem was probably right.

Jem turned to face her properly, and put both hands on her shoulders. His green eyes were solemn. "We might be killed in this adventure, Dora, so I should let you know. I'm not going to marry anyone at all, ever. But if I was going to, it would be you, you dope."

Dora blushed. The hollow feeling had turned into a glorious swoop of delight. But she was not going to give Jem the satisfaction of having the last word.

"Well, I'm not marrying anyone either," she said. "Ever. And you'd *better* not get yourself killed in this adventure, Jem Tollpuddle, because if you do I swear I'll never speak to you again!"

It was as they were sorting out the last bits and pieces of clothing in the kitchen that Caractacus appeared. He flew in the back door like a streak of blue paint and settled on the kitchen table, looking out of breath and waving his tentacles wildly.

"Simon!" he said. "Leaf! We know where he is." There was a pause, as the caterpillar-like creature gathered his breath. "He's in the Roman fort up in Ravenglass!"

"What?" said the Druid. "But he can't be! There's nothing there – no sign of anything. I checked it out completely. Nothing is happening in that area at all!"

"No," said Caractacus frantically. "It's not happening there *now*! It's in the past. He's taken Simon into the fourth century. The crown is being remade in the Roman era!"

The Druid's eyes widened. "Of course!" he said. "That's why the name – the association with Lord Ravenglass in the past has lived on in the name." He clapped his hand to his head. "What an idiot not to see it! You were right, Dora. I should have listened to you."

"But can we go back in time?" said Dora anxiously. "Does this mean we can't reach them?"

The Druid ran his hands through his dark hair, thinking. "Shifting in time can be done," he said slowly. "It's a trickier spell. You need something from the same time and place – from the fort, ideally. And you need a time node."

"A what?" said Jem.

The Druid pulled the flat box towards him from where it was sitting on the table, and started to move his fingers across it, his expression intent. "Time nodes," he said. "They're... sticky places. Time piles up in them. Ever been walking in a wood and suddenly felt it could be a thousand years ago? That it would all still be the same – it wouldn't have changed at all?"

Jem looked blank. "Well, it's always like that. Everywhere. I mean, nothing much changes in the kingdom."

The Druid gave him a crooked grin. "Yes – well, that's true. The kingdom's different, because of the Great Forest. It's virtually all one big node.

But here, there are places that seem to act like bits of the kingdom. They resist change – they let time gather up and just… fold in on itself."

"Wemworthy Heath," said Cat slowly. "That's one, isn't it? There's a dip there, with a stream and some flat stones, and I've sat there before in the sun, on my own, and thought it could have been the Iron Age or something. There would have been the same trees, the same smell of gorse and the sound of the water for all that time…"

"Exactly," said the Druid. "That's what we need, if we want to shift through time. It has to be somewhere where that time still exists, even just a fragment of it. And then you use an object from that point in time to make a portal."

"So could we do it here – on the heath?" said Cat.

Albert frowned. "We could," he said. "But then it would take us about three weeks to get to the old fort on foot. If we didn't get cut to pieces by warring British tribes on the way. Much better to get a fast train to Ravenglass and do the time portal there."

"But don't we still need an object? From Roman times?" said Dora.

The Druid looked up from the flat box, a gleam in his eye. "Indeed we do, Dora. And luckily I've just tracked one down. A silver cup, from the fort itself. Found in a nearby hoard, thirty years ago."

"And where might it be now?" said Albert, with a wary expression.

"It's in the British Museum," said the Druid. He stood up decisively and gestured round the table. "We need to split up. You'd better get off up to Ravenglass, Albert, with the queen and the other heirs. Find a good time node. Get them ready for what they have to do. The rest of us will head to London. We need to get that silver cup and then we'll follow you."

"And how exactly are you proposing to get the cup?" said Albert.

The Druid grinned.

"We're going to steal it," he said.

Chapter Twenty-four

Florence was in charge of the getaway van. She'd driven them into central London in an old Ford Transit that belonged to a friend of a friend of Albert Jemmet. In loud purple paint on the side, the van declared, *Roofs R Us!* and the back was full of bits of guttering, rolls of felt and boxes of slates. Dora and Jem were perched uncomfortably on two of the boxes, hanging on to any available struts whenever Florence flung the van round a sharp corner. Sir Bedwyr was wedged into the other side, sitting on a large bag of loft insulation, and the Druid was up front. The van had no satnav and Florence's mobile was ancient, so he was navigating with a street map. They were nearly in Bloomsbury, and the roads were full of taxis, cycles, cars and buses, all cutting across the lanes as if there was no such thing as driving laws.

"OK, left at the next turning," said the Druid, peering at the map, and then looked up as Florence flicked the indicator down. "*No!* Not that one!"

She veered back into the main road and there was a chorus of horns.

"Er – actually, it *was* that one," he said, craning his neck to see the street sign. "Blast. Umm – next left?"

"No entry," said Florence, through gritted teeth.

"OK, go right here – no right, right! Yes, and then first left – *that* one! The one we've just sailed past. Oh, never mind. Carry on, carry on. *Now* go left!"

The van screeched round the corner into a dead end. Florence had to reverse out into the stream of traffic while a number of people shouted and made rude gestures. The Druid flicked back and forth between a couple of pages and then sent her up the Euston Road, before realising they had to turn round again and take a right into Gower Street.

At last, Florence managed to pull in round the

back of the British Museum, into a space marked *Loading Only*. She hauled on the handbrake, turned the engine off, and took a deep breath. "I am never, *ever*, driving with you again, Lou!" she said. "Not. Ever."

"Yes, well, sorry," said the Druid, peering out of the window. "Haven't been into central London for about ten years. It all looks a bit different from what I remember. But we seem to be in the right place, anyway."

He turned round to look at the others in the back. "OK, we've all got maps of the museum, yes?"

Dora nodded. The Druid had printed out little plans of the rooms in the museum, and given one each to her, Jem and Sir Bedwyr. Each map had the Roman Room circled in red.

"So, do we know what we're doing?"

They nodded again.

"Right – off we go!"

Sir Bedwyr inched his way past the crowd of children that were gathered around a large ornate golden cup in a glass case. Their teacher was explaining its religious significance, while they pushed and strained to get closer.

"It's the Goblet of Fire!" whispered one boy to another at the edge of the crowd.

Sir Bedwyr rolled his eyes. "Useless for a fire," he said sternly to the boy, who looked startled. "Gold. Melts like butter if you try to set a fire in it. Don't they teach you *anything* at your place of apprenticeship?"

He pushed on through the crowd, a tall handsome figure in a dark trench coat, leaving the boys staring after him with puzzled expressions. He could see the double doors ahead of him, leading, according to his printed plan, from Room 41: Medieval Europe to Room 49: Roman Britain. He glanced across at Jem, who was loitering close to the door, and nodded. Jem touched his nose. The signal to wait.

Sir Bedwyr stood in front of the nearest glass case, pretending to be interested in its contents. Then he realised that it was, in fact, a helmet, and became genuinely interested. He frowned at the shadowy eyeholes that stared out at him from a curved metal face. The helmet had heavily decorated eyebrows and a carved moustache below a delicate nosepiece.

"Pretty uncomfortable to wear in battle," he said, looking the helmet up and down carefully. "I mean, covers your head, fine. But there's not much visibility out of those eyeholes."

The woman standing next to him glanced sideways and smiled weakly, before moving off swiftly to the next exhibit.

"Sweaty," said Sir Bedwyr, still brooding on the helmet. He peered at the nose piece. "Not much room in there, either. Awful design. I'd send it straight back to the armoury if they tried to give me anything like that."

He turned, as a man in a black suit moved up to the exhibit. "Don't you agree?" he barked at him, gesturing at the helmet. "Useless in a real fight."

"Er… yes," said the man. "A-absolutely."

Sir Bedwyr peered at him with a frown. He was rather thin, dark and wearing a suit. Was he by any chance another of those crow men? Sir Bedwyr hesitated, and started to feel for the sword strapped to his back, but then he heard a whistle from Jem, and turned back.

Jem was moving purposefully towards the double doors. It was time. Sir Bedwyr gave the man a last hard stare, then strode after Jem. As they reached the doors, the general hum of noise was suddenly replaced with a loud, continuous high-pitched sound, which beat urgently against their ears and rapidly filled the entire gallery space. People started to cry out in panic, and rush in different directions. Jem and Sir Bedwyr put their backs to the double doors, and pointed the other way. The crowd was shouting and pushing, but Sir Bedwyr and Jem held the doors firmly shut.

"Not in here!" roared Sir Bedwyr. "The fire's this way! Get back to the East Stairs!"

"Back to the *other* exit!" shouted Jem. "You need to go the other way!"

People started to turn away, and then a man in museum uniform appeared at the opposite end of the gallery. "This way!" he called. "No need to panic! Orderly evacuation please! Down the East Stairs."

As the crowd started to flow towards the other doors, Jem and Sir Bedwyr looked round carefully, and then slipped into the Roman room. At the other end they could see people filing out of another set of double doors, while the Druid, in a museum uniform, ushered them into Room 50: Europe 800BC–AD43.

"That way!" he called, pointing cheerfully at the doors, which were being held open by Dora. "South stairs to the nearest fire exit!"

The last stragglers shuffled through the doors, and Dora shut them firmly. The gallery was finally empty. They rapidly converged on a glass case near the middle of the room, with a selection of Roman silverware displayed inside. The Druid looked at the case and pushed up the sleeves of his jacket. Putting his hands next to each other on the front of the glass, he closed his eyes and started to move his lips in the words of a spell.

"Where did you get the uniform?" said Jem to Dora. "Nice touch!"

Dora grinned. "Staff cloakroom," she said. "Then we just did a quick smoke spell, set off the alarm. Did you get what we needed from the shop?"

Jem held up a large carrier bag, with *British Museum Gift Shop* printed on the outside, and waved a receipt. "Roman Victrix Beaker," he said, taking out an ornately engraved silver cup. "Nearest thing we could find."

At that moment the Druid managed to make the glass of the cabinet revert to its constituent materials, and a shower of sand, limestone and ash fell through the air and scattered onto the marble floor. Dora reached in and picked up the small silver cup labelled *Roman British Drinking Vessel, Glannaventa Fort, Ravenglass, Cumbria*. She stuffed it into Jem's carrier bag, and placed the replica Victrix beaker in the cabinet. The Druid closed his eyes, and raised his hands, and the scattered bits of sand and grit rose up in the air and coalesced in front of him, sealing the cabinet up again.

"Right," said the Druid, pulling off his museum jacket. "Quick. This way. North stairs, and out to Montague Place. Before they realise it's a false alarm."

They would have got clean away if there hadn't been a particularly zealous security guard posted on the back door. He was new, and his previous job had been as a customs officer. He prided himself on being able to tell when people were trying to smuggle suspicious packages into or out of the country. The two tall, dark men and the two rather strange-looking children accompanying them were, as far as he was concerned, the nearest thing to a terrorist cell he'd seen all lunchtime, and what with the fire alarm going off only five minutes before, and general panic having just been averted, he was not about to let them leave without searching their bags.

"Excuse me, sir," he said, to the older of the two men. "If I could just check your carrier bag?"

"Er, well, yes, of course," said the man, pushing his messy black hair out of his eyes with one hand as he held out the gift shop bag. The security guard gave him a baleful look. *Needs a haircut*, he thought. *Anti-establishment*. He took the silver cup out of the bag and looked at it with slow deliberation.

"What's this, then?" he said.

"Roman Victrix Beaker," said the red-haired boy standing next to them. He waved a receipt. "It's a replica. From the gift shop. Cost a *fortune*."

The guard put his head to one side. "It doesn't look like a replica," he said. "In fact, it doesn't look like the Victrix beaker at all. That's got horses carved on it. Where did you –?"

But he got no further, because the younger man

had pushed him up against the wall and was hissing, "Enough words, peasant! We are on a *mission!*"

The girl grabbed the cup from him, and the four of them pelted out of the back door and up the steps to the street. As the guard staggered after them, shouting for help, he saw them fling themselves into an already revving white van, its back doors wide open. "Go, Florence! GO!" shouted the messy-haired man, and the van engine roared. As the guard stood there, breathless, it screeched down the road, swaying from side to side, and the back doors banged shut as it disappeared round the corner.

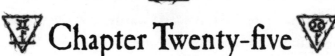

Chapter Twenty-five

It was dark outside by the time the forge was ready. Simon followed Lord Ravenglass down dark stone steps to a rocky cavern that was connected to passages beneath the Praetorium. Smith and Jones had been busy while Ravenglass had been drying off and sampling the latest wine in his quarters above. A bright fire glowed in the furnace to one side of the cavern, the smoke from it twisting up to the high roof and out through a dark fissure in the rock. The fort blacksmith and his assistants had put together a strong workbench and anvil, while the two crow men had unpacked the boxes and organised metals and spell ingredients ready for the making of the crown.

But Simon's eyes were drawn immediately to the figure who was standing across the cavern, watching them all. It seemed the cavern under Glannaventa fort was one of those places and times where a sliver of the world intersected with Lukos's prison. In a sharp line across the rocky floor, Simon could see ice and snow, and behind the invisible barrier, Lukos himself – thin, pale, watchful.

Lukos greeted Simon warily, his blue eyes seeming to bore directly into Simon's brain. *It's Dad*, Simon told himself, hiding the part of him that knew the truth under a pile of trivial nonsense thoughts. *Dad – who gave me my blue elephant when I started playschool, who was there when I played on the grass mound with Alex-with-glasses and Becky-with-plaits, when we had milk with biscuits…*

He squeezed the fear and loathing down, and smiled happily.

"Dad!" he said. "You're here!" He waved his sword. "I helped get the amber from the queen!"

He made his voice as proud as he could, childish, seeking approval. *Just like the day when I found the teacher's lost register and got a gold star, back then when Dad used to collect me from playschool and whirl me round in his arms…*

The man behind the barrier looked at him. Simon felt as if his head was being squeezed in a vice, the pressure gradually increasing till he thought his eyeballs would pop out. Then Lukos smiled.

"Well done, Simon," he said. "I knew we could rely on you."

He turned away with barely a second glance, and Simon breathed out and almost slumped to the floor. But Lukos was now entirely focused on Ravenglass and the jewels he was holding in his hand. He looked different as he stared at them – wilder, fiercer. His voice cracked as he gestured at the amber pieces.

"You have all of them?"

"All of them," said Ravenglass, and stepped right up to the barrier, resting his forehead against it, almost touching the hand that Lukos pressed against the other side, his eyes closed. "We are nearly there."

After a moment, he turned and placed the jewels on the workbench, where they glowed in the reflected light of the forge. He nodded to Mr Smith, who ushered the blacksmith and the remaining soldiers out of the cavern. Mr Jones took charge of the furnace, adding various powders and bits of dried root from the boxes nearby to the flames. They started to leap and dance, strange colours flickering at their heart.

Lord Ravenglass pulled off his velvet coat and rolled his fancy lace shirtsleeves up, revealing surprisingly brawny, tanned arms.

"It's time," he said. "We begin."

For one mad moment, Simon thought of grabbing the amber pieces from the workbench and making a run for it – pelting out of the cavern with them in his hands, conjuring a portal as he ran. But he knew it wouldn't work. Ravenglass could stop him with one outstretched finger – and then he'd be exposed. They'd know he was on the other side. They'd be on their guard, when the others came. And Simon would very probably be dead.

Simon leaned back against the cavern wall, watching the preparations. He stuck his hands in his pockets and felt the feathery comfort of Frizzle's warm body, burrowed down in there, nibbling his hand in a friendly manner. He was glad he had the little creature with him – glad he'd brought him in his hoody when he returned to the kingdom. He felt as if he had a companion with him at least, while he sat there watching Lord Ravenglass slowly and deliberately prepare to destroy all the worlds.

Chapter Twenty-six

Cat was staring out of the train window, wondering what was happening to Simon. She hoped desperately that he was all right. Ever since they'd realised that Simon had gone back to Lord Ravenglass, it was as if a large stone had taken up residence in her stomach. She could feel it there when she swallowed, and it was almost impossible to eat anything. Through all the tension and excitement of the race to get the sea amber, the stone had sat there, indigestible, a reminder that she had failed Simon. Now that she had time to just sit and think, that reminder was almost unbearable. Why hadn't she stopped him? Why hadn't she realised what he was doing? And now he was stuck in the past – in the Roman fort – with Ravenglass, and with the shape-shifter who'd pretended so convincingly to be their father.

She shivered as she remembered those blue eyes, staring at her out of the gaunt face. "It's me, Cat," he'd said. "It's me." And she'd believed him. She clenched her fists, digging her nails into her hand. No wonder Ravenglass had found it easy to re-enchant Simon. Both of them had been so ready to believe, had so wanted it to be Dad. And instead, it was Lukos. Someone Dad had fought against. Someone whose allies he'd helped defeat. And now they had come very close to helping Lord Ravenglass release him.

Opposite Cat, Darien was deep in conversation with Albert Jemmet, who glanced up and gave her a reassuring thumbs up. Queen Igraine was snoring gently in the seat next to her, and Inanna was sprawled across two seats in the next aisle, her head on the table in front of her, her dark braids falling over her face. A young man, squeezed into the seat opposite, was trying to perch his laptop on the very small area of the table that was not currently occupied by Inanna's head or arms. Cat had no idea where Great-Aunt Irene was – she'd turned invisible as soon as they got near

Wemworthy station, and Cat hadn't heard a peep out of her since.

Darien leaned forward, and put a slim brown hand on Cat's arm. "Are you all right?" he said gently. "You look sad."

Cat nearly burst into tears on the spot, but she pressed her lips together and ignored the burning behind her eyes. "Fine," she said. "How long till we get there?"

"Ten minutes," said Albert, glancing at his watch. "Better wake the queen."

Cat gave Queen Igraine a gentle shake and her eyes popped open. She glanced around, confused for a minute, then blinked and nodded to herself. "We're close," she said.

Albert nodded. "Can you feel it?"

The queen made a face. "Not so much feel as smell," she said. "As if the world is burning."

Now she said it, Cat realised that she could sense the same thing. There was a shimmer in the air, like the distortion caused by a heat haze, and she could smell the very faintest trace of smoke.

Albert looked grim. "The spell's advancing," he said. "It's starting to break down the barriers between worlds."

"Will we be in time?" said Cat. "Can we still stop him?"

Queen Igraine put her head to one side, as if listening. "Where are the others?" she said.

Albert pulled out his mobile and looked at the last message he'd got. "They pulled off the M6 half an hour ago," he said. "If we can walk towards the site of the fort, find a time node – they should be close behind us."

Darien reached up to the luggage rack above him and pulled down his fiddle. He plucked a few strings, adjusting the pegs on the neck, and then gave Cat a reassuring grin. "She'll answer to me," he said. "The mermaid's eye. She can't resist a good tune."

Cat nodded. She hoped he was right.

Next to them, Inanna opened her eyes and started to sleepily extract herself from her seat as Albert pulled down his canvas bag. The train rolled slowly into Ravenglass station.

As they emerged onto the main street of Ravenglass, Cat caught her breath in astonishment. The street ran directly alongside an estuary, with nothing the other side of the road but a grassy bank and then flat sand, mud and shingle leading down to the grey water. Sand, mud and water intermingled as far as she could see, sandbanks merging into a grassy low spit of land that stretched across the horizon, with bits of the estuary visible the other side. Further away a dark smudge of land marked the northern shore.

It was a wild, unforgiving place, she thought. Gulls cried overhead, and only a few people could be seen in the growing dusk, walking along the shore or hurrying up the street to their houses.

"Which way?' she said, turning to Albert. He looked around speculatively, then pointed down the road.

"I'm going to say that way," he said. "Along the shore. Get out of the village, see if we can find a bit of deserted beach. Good places for nodes, rivers and beaches. I'll know when I get there."

He set off, a sturdy figure in his blue overalls, Queen Igraine on his arm and Inanna, a little subdued, following close behind. Cat glanced across at Darien.

"Here we go then," she said.

He touched her lightly on her shoulder.

"We'll do our best, Cat," he said. "It's all we can do."

Albert frowned, and peered at the Ordnance Survey map he'd just extracted from his pack.

"Damn," he said. "I think it's the railway that's the problem."

They had tramped half a mile down the beach, away from the village, and as far as Cat could tell, they were in the closest thing to a time node she could imagine. Just sand, scrubby grass and water as far as you could see – no sign of anything man-made.

Albert tapped the map in front of him. "The railway's just behind us. You can't see it, but it's exerting a pull towards this time line. I've known people strong enough to do a shift even so – but it's a hard job. The weight of an iron road is pretty formidable."

He rubbed the back of his bald head, thinking, and then pointed off to one side. "There's a path – takes us under the railway line and up into some woods. Might be that's our best bet."

Queen Igraine sighed and took his arm

again. "My poor old bones," she said with a grimace, and held out her other hand to Inanna. "Come, my dear. You can tell me all about your kingdom as we walk. It sounds fascinating. And your goddess. I'd love to visit, once all this is over."

Inanna took her hand gratefully, and her dark eyes brightened as she started to tell the queen all about life in Ur-Akkad, and the many duties of a priestess-daughter of the mighty Sargon.

"She's very good, isn't she?" came an approving voice from over Cat's left shoulder. Cat jumped, and turned to see the silvery outline of Great-Aunt Irene. "I mean, Inanna's clearly terrified," the ghostly figure went on. "Still hasn't really got the hang of sending her magic, and she knows it. Igraine might seem a bit old and dotty sometimes, but she's found exactly the right way to calm Inanna down."

"Yes, I suppose so," said Cat, watching the two of them heading up the footpath together, alongside Albert's stocky figure. "Umm – have you been behind me long?"

"Since we got off the train," said Great-Aunt Irene, solidifying slightly. "Of course, I had to stay invisible in the carriage. Bit inconvenient, really. I had the tea trolley pushed right through me twice. *Not* a very comfortable sensation, I can assure you. So we're looking for a node?"

"Yes," said Cat. "Albert seems to think – up there in the woods…"

"Well, better get a move on, then," said Great-Aunt Irene, drifting rapidly up the path. "We really haven't got very long. I hope Florence and Lou are on their way."

Cat pulled out her mobile and checked it again, for the twentieth time since they'd arrived in Ravenglass village. No message. She headed off up the path after Great-Aunt Irene, her fingers typing as she went. *Where r u? R u nearly here?*

"It's Cat again," said Jem, peering at the mobile phone display, which was lit up with a green glow in the growing darkness of the van. "They've found a good node. She wants to know when we'll be there."

"Tell her we're nearly in Ravenglass," said Florence, frowning at the road in front of her. "Or at least, I think we are…"

A sign flashed past and she braked. "Did that

say Ravenglass?" she said, turning to Dora.

"I – er – I don't think so," said Dora. "It started with an H, I think."

Florence glanced in her rear-view mirror and cautiously reversed. As the sign reappeared they could all see the dark lettering picked out in the van's headlights: Holmrook. Florence banged her hands down on the steering wheel in frustration. "We've missed it," she said. "Too far. I'll have to turn round."

She leaned back over the seat and squinted into the back of the van. "Lou? How are you doing back there?"

"Getting there," came a muffled voice. Dora could just see a shadowy outline bent over between the boxes of roof tiles and bags of insulation. The Druid was twisting some kind of rope out of bits of wool, with broken pieces of slate attached at intervals. As he tied the bits of wool together, he was muttering spells of binding and warding. They had no idea how close they would be to Ravenglass, or Lukos, when they shifted, and the Druid was not taking any chances. He wanted them all inside the strongest warding he could manufacture, one that would travel with them to the past, so it had to be made of natural materials like wool and slate – of which, luckily, there was an abundance in the back of Albert's friend's van.

The van lurched suddenly and Florence pulled into a layby and hauled on the handbrake.

"It's here," she said, and turned the engine off. They all peered round at each other in the sudden gloom.

"Right ho!" said Sir Bedwyr, unfolding himself from the corner, where he had been carefully wedged. "This is it, then."

He opened the back door and clambered stiffly out, then stretched and pulled his sword out from under his coat. It was a clear, cold night and the sword gleamed in the pale light of a half-moon, sailing above the trees. Jem climbed out after him and peered at the mobile in his hand. He pointed down the narrow footpath that led into the trees.

"Cat says they're in the middle of the woods. Should be that way," he said, and set off up the path, the others following him.

They were all gathered together in a clearing in the woods, the moonlight filtering down through the trees, the whole place still and quiet. Cat was standing close to Florence, and they were both watching the Druid, who had his eyes closed. His crooked face was intently focused, and he stood completely still. The makeshift rope of wool and slate was laid out around them in a rough circle and inside it they all stood, shoulder to shoulder, weapons at the ready and magic, if they had it, tingling at their fingertips.

The Druid opened his eyes. "The cup, Jem?" he said, and Jem handed over the gift shop bag. Pulling the cup out, the Druid gave them all an encouraging grin. "You might feel a bit sick," he said, and then held up the cup and started to say the words of the spell.

Cat watched as the cup started to glow, and then their surroundings started to break up, like a jigsaw puzzle coming apart, the pieces whirling around them. She felt as if she were plummeting down a deep hole, and almost put her arms out to stop herself falling, but she was wedged in by Jem on one side and Florence on the other. It was like stepping through a portal while being catapulted round a fairground ride, she thought, trying very hard not to throw up all over Jem's feet.

At last, as suddenly as it had begun, the

whirling stopped and the jigsaw pieces rearranged themselves into exactly the same pattern as before.

"Did we actually go anywhere?" said Jem, his hand over his mouth, his face white.

The Druid, shaking slightly and panting, nodded his head. "It's the right time – the right hour," he gasped. "As we were travelling back, I could feel it, like a great magnet, pulling us in. It's pulling all times towards it at the moment. All places, for that matter. Like a huge black hole. We're very close to the end."

Chapter Twenty-seven

The walls of the fort loomed up in the darkness, the glow of a brazier illuminating the main gates where the guards sat stamping their feet and blowing on their hands.

"*Provincia pessima est. Digiti gelantur,*" muttered one in a disgruntled voice.

Another of the men laughed. "*Ita – et plenus barballis et ovibus.*"

"*Provinciam odeo,*" the first growled, holding his hands over the fire.

Dora frowned. What had they said? She looked at the Druid, who seemed unaware that anything was wrong, and was striding forward confidently.

"*Salvete, milites!*" he said cheerfully. "*Nuntium centurioni castri habemus!*"

"What the…?" hissed Jem, coming up behind

Dora. "He's speaking a different language! What happened to the portal magic?"

"I don't know," Dora whispered. "It's not working. We'd better not say anything till we've worked out what to do about it."

The Druid was chatting happily with the soldiers, who were completely unaware of the goodwill spell he was weaving as he spoke to them.

"*Ah, ita, ita, nobiscum venite!*" one of them said with a cheery smile, waving with a gesture of welcome. "*Omnis barballi hic excipiuntur!*"

The Druid beckoned the others into the fort, and gradually they filed past the guards, who nodded at them in a slightly dazed but friendly manner. Once they were safely past, Dora plucked at the Druid's sleeve.

"We can't understand a word they're saying!" she said, in a low voice. "The language magic didn't work!"

The Druid looked at her in consternation. "You mean I was actually speaking Latin from memory?" he said. "That's not good news – it means the remaking is far enough advanced to have affected the portal magic. I'd better see about the rest of you."

He extended his hand and muttered a few words. Dora felt a tingling on her tongue. "Has that worked?" she said, but she knew as soon as she spoke that it had. Her mouth felt odd, as if it had too many teeth, and the sounds coming out of it were not quite normal, although she understood them perfectly.

"It's this way," he said, in a low voice, but Dora thought he hardly needed to say anything. Ever since they'd entered the fort she'd been intensely aware of the spell that was being worked up ahead. It was pulling them forward, burning through the darkness like a molten star. Glancing at the others, she could see that they, too, could feel it, even the ones with no magic.

They hurried up the street until they found themselves at the centre of the fort, in a large square with imposing stone buildings. There was a dark, narrow alley along the side of one of the buildings, and it pulled at them like a magnet. But as they entered, and saw the shadowy archway where the pull was coming from, it started to seem increasingly as if they were wading through water. Each step seemed harder to take, and around them the darkness began to solidify. Soldiers suddenly appeared behind them at the end of the alley, but they, too, were moving slowly – not quite frozen, but slowed, as if they were insects caught in treacle.

Dora started to feel scared. Had Ravenglass succeeded in making the crown and freeing Lukos? Was this what it felt like – the breaking down of the world's bounds? Was this time itself running out, like sand from an hour glass?

"Lou!" cried Florence, behind her. "What's happening?"

The Druid grimaced. "Barrier spell," he said through clenched teeth. "Give me a minute. Igraine – if you could help – and Dora. It might take all of us."

He held out one hand to the queen and took Dora's in his other. She let her magic flow through her hand, adding to the counter-magic the Druid was building up, feeling it expand outwards like a wave crashing through the sticky air around them. As it swept across them, they found they could move – but so could the soldiers behind them. And now there was a clanging of bells from all corners of the fort and shouts of alarm.

"That's torn it," said the Druid. He whipped

out his sword and looked round wildly. Soldiers were arriving from every direction, rushing across the square towards them.

Sir Bedwyr clapped him on the shoulder. "Time for those with fighting skills to do their part," he said. "Let's see if we can hold this little lot off, give you some time. Come on, Jem – swords out!"

Whirling his sword over his head, he charged at the soldiers heading up the alleyway and started setting about him with gusto. Jem pulled out his short sword and, with a reassuring grin at Dora, followed him.

The Druid nodded to Queen Igraine. "Ravenglass is down there," he said. "I can feel the magic taking hold. We'll do our best to hold the soldiers off – but it's down to you now. It's down to the heirs."

As Cat stepped into the shadow of the archway, she saw the Druid, sword in one hand, the other stretched out to send a few stunning spells at the oncoming soldiers. Dora was frowning and weaving protective magic around Jem and Sir Bedwyr. And Mum – Mum! – was holding a sword in two hands and standing firmly next to

Great-Aunt Irene, telling the soldiers not to come any closer to her daughter if they wanted to live to see another sunrise.

Cat slipped further into the dark passageway, and felt Darien's hand on her arm, pulling her towards a set of stairs.

"He's down there," said Queen Igraine in a low voice. She and Inanna were right behind them. "Those ghastly crow men too. But only them. Are we ready?"

They glanced at each other, and moved instinctively closer together. The queen looked at them all gravely.

"Whatever happens in there," she said, "we concentrate on the amber. Cat – to the east – the earth amber. Darien – to the west. Inanna, my dear – you'll be south. Just opposite me, if you can." She drew herself up. "I shall be in the north. I shall be taking back the power of the sky amber from that rotten, double-dealing scoundrel. And –" she looked suddenly fierce, and Cat could see the power singing through every bone in her body – "*you* will all be doing the same." She leaned over and touched Inanna on the shoulder. "Especially *you*, my girl. You have more magic than you think. You're holding back at the moment – trying not to set anything on fire. Well, right now, fire's the least of our worries. So let it all go. *All* your power. Wrap the fire amber in flames so hot he simply won't be able to hold it any longer."

Inanna nodded solemnly, and Cat could see from the gleam in her eye that she'd lost her fear. She was going to give it everything she had, and Cat had a suspicion that everything Inanna had would turn out to be quite a considerable amount of power.

She glanced sideways at Darien and he tucked his fiddle under his chin and raised his bow.

"Ready?" he said.

She took a deep breath and nodded. She *was* ready, she realised. Now it came to it, she was more than ready. Simon was down there and he needed to be rescued. Lukos was down there, and instead of fear she just felt overwhelming anger. He'd tricked them. He'd pretended *to be their dad*. She was damned if he was going to get away with that. She was taking the earth amber – her amber – back into her power and he was *not* going to stop her.

Chapter Twenty-eight

The furnace at the heart of the forge glowed like a small red sun.

Mr Smith was pumping the bellows, Mr Jones stoking the fire. Lord Ravenglass was working a newly forged length of Old Iron, his hands enclosed in leather gloves. Sweat trickled down his handsome face, and his dark ringlets hung damply round his shoulders. He was hammering the iron, which was rapidly cooling from white hot to a dull red colour, twisting and turning it with a pair of heavy tongs, holding it up and then bending again over the anvil, hammering some more. He raised his right arm and dabbed the sweat off his face with his shirtsleeves, then flung the iron back into the furnace to reheat.

"Water," he said, gesturing to Simon to hand

him a nearby jug. He drank deeply, then wiped his mouth with the back of his hand and grinned. His eyes were burning into Simon's, his face alight with something more than just the reflected light of the flames.

"So close," he said, and laughed. He clapped Simon on the back. "Can you feel it?" he said. "Can you feel the magic taking hold?"

Simon nodded. He could indeed feel it. He'd felt it ever since Ravenglass had started forging the crown – murmuring spells over the iron bands as he bent and twisted them, gradually bringing the metal round in a perfect circle, tweaking the smaller lengths out into the spiky clasps that would hold the pieces of amber. It was as if the world around them was getting smaller, falling into itself, being pulled gradually into a single point – here and now, in this rocky cavern beneath a Roman fort. Simon could see flickering images at the edges of his vision – people, animals, buildings – he could hear the murmur of voices, the crash of waves, the creak of timbers – moments of other times and places appearing and disappearing as the bounds of the worlds weakened.

Only one place remained utterly constant. A few short paces from the glow of Ravenglass's forge, the tall figure of Lukos was standing pressed against the invisible barrier, the silver chains binding his limbs stretched out behind him. He had been watching intently as the iron being worked by Ravenglass gradually took shape into a circlet of intertwined bands.

Ravenglass bent over the anvil again, sweat beading once more on his face as he started to work on the last setting. Beside him, Mr Smith carefully picked up the orange-brown earth amber and placed it in the middle of the iron workbench on which the anvil sat.

"It's time," he hissed, with a malevolent glance at Simon.

"Indeed it is," said Lord Ravenglass, straightening up and beckoning Simon towards him. "This is where you do your bit, Simon. This is where you help to save your father."

Simon fingered the hilt of his sword with one hand. "Wh-what do you need me to do?" he asked, his throat suddenly very dry.

Lord Ravenglass gestured at the earth amber, nestled in its elaborate clasp of twisting bronze leaves, and gave him an encouraging pat on the back. "We need you to cut the amber from its clasp, my dear boy. Each piece must be released from the clasp before we can meld its full power with the crown. And only Bruni's sword, wielded by Bruni's heir, will do the trick."

He grinned at Simon, and waggled one long elegant finger. "You *did* say you'd do anything we needed you to. Well, this is it."

Simon nodded, trying to think rapidly. If he didn't cut the amber from its clasps, did that mean they couldn't reforge the crown? Would that be enough to stop them?

He moved slowly towards the workbench, pulling the sword out of its makeshift buckle. Pressed against the barrier nearby, Lukos was staring at him hungrily.

Simon raised the sword, and measured the distance to the jewel lying in front of him on the flat anvil. What should he do? Where were the others? Were they coming? He could stall, go as slowly as possible – but would they be here in time?

Ravenglass gestured impatiently, and Simon brought the sword down. There was a flash of bright light as it hit the anvil. The amber, free of its clasp, rolled onto the bench, while the bronze leaves that had held it were scattered, their colour suddenly dull, lifeless.

Immediately Ravenglass seized the amber and inserted it into one of the settings on the crown, twisting the metal with his heavy tongs till it held the orange-brown stone firmly in place. He spoke a number of words as he twisted, and the iron of the crown seemed to take on a faint glow. A pulse of power swept outwards across the cavern.

"I can feel it," said Lukos, his eyes burning. "The walls – they're weakening."

Mr Smith placed the fire amber on the anvil, its glowing heart surrounded by the golden flames of the clasp.

"And again, Simon, if you please," said Ravenglass, holding the crown ready to take its second piece of amber.

Simon swallowed. Should he refuse? But then they'd know he'd broken the spell. He'd be in terrible danger. *The others are coming*, he said to himself. *They'll be here soon*. He lifted the sword and brought it down again, releasing the fire amber. Ravenglass bound it swiftly into the crown as he spoke the words of the binding spell. Mr Smith slapped the sea amber onto the anvil and looked expectantly at Simon. The mermaid's green eye winked up at him, its copper clasp still embedded in a surround of dark wood.

Slowly, reluctantly, Simon cut the sea amber from the copper and wood that held it. The crown was almost made – and as Ravenglass bound the sea amber into place with a third spell, the circlet seemed to sing with power.

Lukos beat his fists against the barrier, his expression triumphant. "We're nearly there. I can *taste* it!" He was barely bothering to appear any more as Gwyn Arnold. His eyes were narrower, flecked with yellow, his hair darker, his face thinner and sharper. And his teeth – Simon shivered. They were pointed, like the teeth of an animal, his lips drawn back almost in a snarl.

Ravenglass wiped his face with the back of his sleeve, and grinned at Lukos. "Patience," he said. "One more to go."

Mr Smith placed the sky amber on the anvil. It shone brightly, the silver threads of its clasp twisting around the orange stone and gleaming with a myriad of reflected colours.

Simon stared at the amber, his mind racing. This was the last one – his last chance to stop the making of the crown. There was no sign of the others, no rescue party clattering down the stone steps. It was up to him.

"No," he said, reversing his grip on the sword so that it pointed downwards, as if he meant to drive the blade into the rocky floor of the cavern. "I won't do it. I won't cut the clasp."

Lord Ravenglass looked at Simon, one eyebrow raised. "So," he said. "I did wonder. Mr Smith? Mr Jones? If you would."

Swift as thought, Smith and Jones were at Simon's side. They gripped his arms, and cold seeped into his body from the places where they held him. Their faces were pushed up close to his, their black eyes boring into his.

"Broke the spell, did we?" rasped Mr Jones into one ear.

"What a naughty boy," whispered Mr Smith into the other.

Lord Ravenglass pointed at the sky amber on its anvil. "Very noble of you, Simon, to try and stop me. But to no avail, I'm afraid. The amber must be cut using Bruni's sword, wielded by

Bruni's heir. But there's nothing in the magic to say it must be wielded *willingly*."

He nodded at the two crow men, and Simon felt them grip his shoulders tightly. His sword arm started moving of its own accord. He willed it to stop, willed it to stay by his side, but his whole arm and shoulder felt numb, icy, and he couldn't open his fingers to drop the sword. The blade flashed in the light of the furnace and Simon watched in despair as it came down on the sky amber, shattering the silver clasp into tiny pieces.

Mr Jones wrenched the sword out of his hand and threw it to the ground, and Lord Ravenglass picked up the amber. He gave Simon a deep bow. "My thanks," he said. "Even if you did need a little encouragement at the end."

"Oh yes," said Mr Smith, patting Simon's shoulder. "A little encouragement…"

"… from your friends," finished Mr Jones, tweaking Simon's ear with his long white fingers.

"Shall we kill him now?" they said together, looking at Ravenglass.

"Yes," said Ravenglass, then frowned, his head to one side. "No, wait. I'll do it myself."

Ravenglass pointed one hand at Simon and

sent a fierce spell sizzling across the cavern. Simon felt as if he'd been hit by a charging bull. The rocky floor of the cave slammed into his back and all the breath was knocked out of his body. His eyelids fluttered, and everything went black.

Chapter Twenty-nine

There was a blinding pain behind Simon's eyes and he could feel the stony ground pressing into his cheek. He moved his head and then gasped as a thousand needles seemed to skewer every inch of his body. Across from him, he could see Lord Ravenglass bending over the crown, twisting the last pieces of metal round the sky amber. He must have been unconscious for only a few seconds.

"There's counter-magic brewing," snarled Lukos suddenly. He lifted his head, sniffed at the air, pushed at the barrier, the tendons of his neck standing out with tension. He pointed one long white finger at Ravenglass. "There's trouble coming. See to the crown – now! Before it's too late! *Don't fail me, Ravenglass!*"

Ravenglass glanced backwards at the steps out

of the cavern, and gestured to Smith and Jones. The two dark figures strode across the cavern, hands raised, conjuring magic as they walked, while Ravenglass, with a frown of concentration, twisted the clasp around the sky amber and said the last words of the making spell.

A sound like the splitting of a great tree trunk filled the cavern. Fighting for breath, Simon saw the crown begin to change shape. The dark iron was splitting and dividing, tendrils twisting tighter around the four bits of amber. Leaves were sprouting from the metal as if it were living wood, unfurling and curling protectively around the amber pieces. When the movement stopped, the crown was glowing with the golden warmth of the Great Tree, the four jewels nestled like fruit in amongst the metal leaves. It was beautiful, and awesome.

Simon felt tears gathering at the corners of his eyes. The amber crown. It was made. They were too late.

Ravenglass lifted the crown and placed it on his head – but there was a growing commotion at the cavern entrance. Smith and Jones were being beaten backwards by a storm of magic from the passageway beyond. As they retreated, Simon could see that the magic was coming from four figures, doggedly pushing forward into the cavern.

He squinted through the smoky half-light and felt a burst of joy. It was Cat! And Inanna! They were hurling spells at the two crow men, while the queen, next to them, reached out her hand towards Ravenglass. Next to her, a tall, dark-skinned young man was drawing a bow across an old fiddle tucked under his chin, and the cavern was suddenly filled with an eerie, haunting tune that echoed off the walls.

Ravenglass backed towards the ice barrier, looking wildly at Lukos.

"Do the spell!" snarled Lukos. "Get me out of here! I can deal with this lot with one hand tied behind my back. *If* you get me out!"

Ravenglass nodded and drew himself up. He started to declaim the words of the unbinding spell, the spell that would dissolve all the barriers between worlds and finally release the Lord of Wolves. They were sonorous words, words that got inside Simon's head and seemed to reverberate, like a great bell clanging against his skull. Word after word Ravenglass spoke, the notes piling onto each other, building up, vibrating through his body. Simon put his hands to his head. He could see Cat flinching, and Inanna stuffing her fingers into her ears.

Then, a light, dancing tune started to weave through the layers of sound, a trickle of notes like a bubbling stream flowing over and round and through the great echoing words of the spell, somehow pushing them back, deadening their effect. Simon lifted his head and saw the young man with the fiddle, stepping gracefully over to one side of the cavern, his fingers dancing along the neck, his feet tapping in time to the tune, his eyes fixed intently on the crown on Ravenglass's head. Some of the glow seemed to be fading from the crown, and Ravenglass was sweating as he continued to force out the words of the spell, his face as white as the snow in Lukos's prison.

Smith and Jones glanced across at the young man and then at each other. Together they turned, ready to leap at him. But there was a clattering sound from the passageway and a shout: "No you don't!" Suddenly Albert Jemmet was there, in the cavern, his bald head glowing in the light of the furnace, his sword out in front of him. Behind him, Sir Bedwyr crashed into the cavern at full tilt, heading straight for Mr Jones, and then it was Jem, flying across the ground and making a grab for Mr Smith's legs. And behind them all, Great-Aunt Irene and the Druid, with rather a lot of blood pouring down his face, leaning on... Mum! It was Mum! Simon felt his heart leap. She was holding the Druid upright and scouring the cavern anxiously, a sword held purposefully in her right hand, and when she saw him, her face lit up with a joyful smile.

Simon rolled over onto his hands and knees, breathing heavily. He gathered as much magic as he could and tried to use it to shake off the remnants of whatever spell Ravenglass had used on him. Gradually, he began to feel more in control, his mind clearing, the life coming back into his limbs.

Cat was standing nearby, opposite the young man with the fiddle. She had a fierce look on her face as she concentrated on taking back control of the earth amber. Queen Igraine was standing close to the ice barrier, her hand outstretched towards Ravenglass. Inanna, opposite the queen, had a smile playing around her lips, her face lit up with a glow of power. Around the four figures the air shimmered, enclosing them in a circle of crackling magic with Ravenglass at the centre.

The crown's light was fading – but Ravenglass, drenched in sweat, was still murmuring the words of the unbinding spell. Lukos, his fists clenched, his expression intent, was declaiming them with him, word after word, the ringing sounds beating against Simon's head like hammer blows.

Ravenglass's face was rigid with tension. As the light of the crown faded, the glow of the four pieces of amber was increasing. The fire amber was like a fragment of the setting sun boring through the metal of the crown. Ravenglass winced, and as he did so, Inanna laughed and raised her hands and the amber was suddenly surrounded by dancing flames. The notes of the young man's fiddle were louder now, wilder, and the sea amber was twinkling like a merry hazel eye peeping out of the leaves of the crown. Ravenglass gritted his teeth and carried on, but now the earth amber was alight, twisting golden glints writhing in its depths, and the queen's amber, the sky amber of the kingdom, was like a star shining out from beneath the dark tendrils of iron that were wreathed around it.

Ravenglass spat out the last words of the spell with a gasp, and the world shivered.

Everything stopped.

Chapter Thirty

The crown had the faintest glow along the tendrils of iron. The four figures surrounding Ravenglass stood firm, using all their power to control the four pieces of amber. They were holding them back, slowing the magic, but it couldn't be reversed. The barriers of Lukos's prison started to shimmer. The silver chains on his arms and legs started to stretch and fade. He held out his arms slowly, intently, and pushed them through the barrier as if through a wall of mist.

Simon felt a hand on his shoulder, felt the hilt of his sword pushed into his hand.

Dora had crept across the cavern, unseen by anyone, and picked up the sword where it had been dropped by Mr Smith. Now she was gripping Simon hard on the arm, and pushing him towards

Lord Ravenglass, her face white but her brown eyes steady.

"Quick!" she said. "Break it!"

Simon barely had time to think about what he was about to do. He raised the sword, and threw himself at Lord Ravenglass. For an instant, their eyes met. Ravenglass looked startled – desperate – and then the sword flashed down.

But Lord Ravenglass was no longer there. As the blade descended, he seemed to fold in on himself, becoming smaller, darker, denser. The crown fell to the floor, and Simon's sword crashed through it with a ringing sound, cutting it into two pieces. But the dark shape that had been Lord Ravenglass was now swirling round the cavern. As it passed over Smith and Jones, they also melted into two knots of shadow and suddenly there were three crows, diving across the roof of the cavern, shrieking in anger.

The Druid raised his arms and spoke the words of a spell. The crows were picked up as if by a hurricane and hurled, wings flapping desperately, into the ice world. Lukos was howling, less of a man now and more of a wolf, his teeth longer, sharper, yellower, his eyes raging with anger. But the crown was broken, and now the barrier was no longer just mist, and the silver chains were growing stronger, tighter. Lukos and the crows were being pulled backwards into a whirl of snow, and suddenly the whole ice world itself began to shimmer. Simon glanced across and saw that Queen Igraine had picked up the two halves of the amber crown and was reaching out with them towards Lukos, all four jewels glowing brightly as she banished the icy prison from the fort. Lukos, the crows and the whirling snow began to disappear, getting smaller and smaller until there was nothing but dark rock walls where they had been.

There was a moment of shocked silence, and then Queen Igraine nodded with satisfaction.

"It's done," she said. "Lukos is back in his prison, and the worlds are safe."

Florence strode across the cavern and wrapped Simon up in a fierce hug. Cat joined them, and then Florence held out one hand to the Druid, and he took it and beamed at them. Simon saw Dora pat Inanna on the back and Jem punch Sir Bedwyr's shoulder, and Albert put the bits of crown safely in his backpack and then take Queen Igraine by the hands and whirl her round.

But their celebrations were interrupted by a resounding crash from above and the sound of shouts and people running. Jem lifted his head and sniffed.

"I can smell smoke," he said. "Inanna? Do you think you might have set fire to the fort?"

Inanna had indeed set fire to the fort. As they staggered out of the cavern they could all smell the smoke, and the glow of flames flickered on the stone walls of the Praetorium. The wooden barracks were ablaze and most of the soldiers were too busy running around with buckets of water or salvaged equipment to pay them any attention.

"This way," said Albert, ushering them further down the alley. "There'll be a back gate. There's always a back gate."

They stumbled through the darkness, trying to avoid the soldiers, ducking through smoky passageways and flinching from the occasional bit of burning building that crashed down in front of them. Florence was almost knocked flying by a falling beam, and the Druid had to conjure a swift spell to put out the flames, but other than that they made it through the fort without incident. Once at the gate, they slipped out into the darkness by the river. The mingled shouts, the crash of collapsing barracks and the crackle of flames faded behind them as they made their way along the shore.

"Here," said Simon. "This is the place where we arrived."

He could see a couple of boxes from the palace, emptied of goods, left stacked by the grassy bank. The place had a quiet, timeless quality about it, the water lapping at the shore, the bank a smudgy shadow in the moonlight.

Albert frowned. "We could try from here – but it's not ideal… It's where the railway line will be in the future."

"It doesn't matter," said the Druid, who was kneeling by the water's edge, splashing his face and trying to rinse some of the blood out of his hair. "It won't affect us going in the opposite direction. In fact, it might help. It'll pull us towards the right time."

Albert considered, then nodded. "You're right. OK – have we got any metal objects, people? Preferably nice and modern."

Cat fumbled in her pocket and held out her phone. "Will this do? It's just been upgraded."

Darien took it from her, and turned it in his hand, quizzically.

"It's a mobile," said Cat. "For communicating with someone far away. You dial their number, and then you talk…"

He grinned at her. "So – when I get back to the Adamantine Sea, you can speak to me… with your mobile?"

Cat started to giggle. "And then we could," she hiccupped, "have a chat? And maybe – oh, I don't know… go on a date?"

Darien's eyes gleamed in his dark face. "As you say. On a date. Whatever that might be. Or we could go somewhere… peaceful. Perhaps with some wine and nice things to eat."

"She's only fourteen," said Florence swiftly. "She's not allowed to drink."

Simon looked at Cat's dirty, smudged face, the smears of blood on the Druid, his mum's scorched clothes and frazzled expression, then at Darien's hopeful face and back at Cat, giggling hysterically. He found himself dissolving into laughter. Next to him, Dora's shoulders started to shake, and then Jem bent over, his hands on his knees, gulping. Sir Bedwyr, leaning on his sword, smiled indulgently, and Inanna started to giggle as well.

"We did it," said Simon, between gulps of laughter. "We actually did it."

Queen Igraine, her white hair in some degree of disarray, her face smeared with soot, smiled round at them all. "We did," she agreed. "We made the worlds safe. Two old ladies, a ragbag assortment of children, an odd-job man and some fellow travellers. The blessings of the forest on us all."

"Hear, hear!" said Albert with a grin, as he took Cat's mobile in his hand. "Better hang on to each other," he added, and he conjured the shift.

The beach around them dissolved into a kaleidoscope of patterns and colours. Simon pressed his lips together, holding on to his mum with one hand and Cat with the other. As the world settled down again, the estuary came into focus, glinting in the faint light of the half-moon. Simon took a deep breath.

"We're back," he said.

Albert fished a golden forest leaf out of his pocket and held it up. "One more shift," he said. "We need to get to the forest. It's time the pieces of deep amber were returned to the Tree."

Chapter Thirty-one

The Great Tree glowed, its branches twisting around each other and reaching up into the swirling white mists of other worlds. Dora caught her breath as she looked at it, the power of the Tree humming through the whole clearing, the dappled light bathing them all in a golden haze.

She turned to Simon. "It's beautiful!"

He nodded. "I know. It's like the amber, isn't it? You can see it's alive." He pulled Frizzle out of his pocket, and held the small creature up. "Look, Frizzle! It's the Great Tree!"

Frizzle chirruped happily, his little black eyes bright, then hopped onto Simon's shoulder and burrowed into the neck of his jumper.

"You know, he probably saved your life," said

the Druid, coming over and tickling Frizzle under the chin.

The Druid was looking much better, Dora thought. The blood had been washed off and he had clean, dry clothes, but it was more than that. It was the relief that they'd made it through, that the job was done and they were all alive. She felt it, too – they all did. There was a lightness and glow in the faces in the clearing that had nothing to do with the reflected light of the Great Tree.

"Saved my life?" said Simon. "How?"

"They have a primitive magic of their own, margravets. It's a protective magic that reduces a spell's effect. Frizzle would have activated it when Ravenglass's spell hit you both, last night. I'm guessing it's why you survived. Frizzle reduced its power."

"He shielded me from the spell?" said Simon with surprise. "But I felt like I'd been run over by a bus!"

The Druid clapped him on the shoulder. "Well, he wouldn't have had strong enough magic to ward you completely. But the full spell was undoubtedly meant to kill you."

Simon looked at the little creature wonderingly.

So Frizzle had saved him – prevented Ravenglass from finishing him off. He stroked the small bundle of feathers, and Frizzle purred.

"He saved us all, then, if you think about it," said Cat. "Because if Simon hadn't been there, the crown wouldn't have been destroyed."

"Indeed," said Great-Aunt Irene, materialising behind them in her ghostly way. "So we have to thank your foolish experiments with portals for the continuing existence of the worlds as we know them."

"Funny thing, eh?" said Albert, his thumbs stuck in his belt loops, gazing at the Tree. "You never know what's going to turn out to be important in the end, do you?"

As he spoke, a small blue creature whizzed into the clearing and settled itself on a nearby branch.

"Finally got yourselves clean and sorted?" Caractacus said, waving his tentacles. "Because we need to get on with the business at hand."

He gestured to the Tree, where they could suddenly see a number of the tall, green-brown tree guardians. As they looked over, one of the tree-like figures detached himself from the group, and walked towards them.

"Rowan," said Cat in greeting.

"Catrin," he said, inclining his head gracefully. "Simon. All of you. We are forever grateful for what you did. But we must ask you now to relinquish the ambers. To let them go back to the Tree, so the crown can never be remade again. Lukos will be fixed in his ice world forever, and the worlds of light will finally be safe."

Cat nodded, a little sadly, and she, Queen Igraine, Darien and Inanna all stepped forward. They had prised their pieces of amber out of the remnants of the crown. Now they held the amber jewels out to Rowan, straight-backed, determined, but each with the same ache of loss in their face.

He took them, one by one, into his green-brown hand: the sparkle of the kingdom's sky amber, the gleam of the sea amber, the orange-brown earth amber with twisting gold flecks in its depths, and finally the red glow of Inanna's fire amber. A tear dripped gently off Cat's nose as she watched Rowan walk back to the Tree with the four pieces in his hand.

Darien nudged her. "Some of their magic remains," he said. "We'll always have it, within us."

She sniffed, and nodded.

He lifted up his fiddle, tucked it under his chin and started to play, as Rowan handed pieces of amber to three other Guardians and together they took up positions around the Tree: east, west, south and north. The notes of Darien's fiddle floated across the clearing, tangling with the branches of the Great Tree, dancing with the golden leaves, making everyone's feet twitch.

The four Guardians stepped forward and the pieces of amber started to shine fiercely as they touched the golden trunk of the Tree. For a moment, their brightness was almost unbearable. Then they started to draw themselves in, the glow of each becoming part of the glow of the Tree. The branches shivered and the Tree seemed to increase in size, its power suddenly so clear and awesome that Cat could hardly breathe – and then the deep ambers were gone, and there was just the Tree, its quiet golden light filling the clearing.

"It's done," said Darien, as he drew his bow across the strings of his violin with a final, haunting chord, and then he dropped his hands.

The rest of the day passed in a whirl of food, drink, music, dancing and celebration. Dora had no idea who half the people were who arrived to enjoy the magnificent feast Caractacus had organised. Forest agents, tree guardians, dignitaries and royalty from half the worlds over. Queen Igraine presided, and Caractacus bustled around making sure everyone was behaving themselves. Dora and the others found their hands aching from being pressed and their jaws hurting from too much smiling. As Dora nodded and bobbed yet another curtsey to another First Minister, she felt a hand pulling at her sleeve.

"Dora!" hissed Jem. "Over here!"

She made her excuses to the First Minister and then followed Jem down a narrow path between two thorny trees. Eventually he led her to a small, quiet clearing where she found the others. They had managed to escape from the celebrations, bringing a considerable proportion of the feast with them.

Cat waved at her from her perch on an old tree stump, her legs stretched out in front of her. Simon was lying on his back on the grass, his head on her feet, and Inanna was leaning against the same tree stump. Near her, Sir Bedwyr was lying propped up on one arm, explaining the finer points of jousting.

Dora grinned at them, and turned to the Druid and Albert, who were sitting with Florence by a small campfire with dancing flames.

"Have a marshmallow," said the Druid, holding up a stick with a melted pink and brown blob on the end.

Dora looked at it doubtfully, then picked the pink blob up in her fingers and put it in her mouth.

Jem laughed at her expression. "Good, aren't they?" he said, picking up a stick and fixing a white blob on the end before holding it in the flames. "We'll have to import a few bags from Simon's world to have in the forest."

Dora chewed, letting the sweetness spread over her tongue, and then swallowed.

"In the forest?" she said. "Is that where we're staying?"

Albert looked up at her with a grin. "If you want to, Dora. You're a fine witch. Just the sort of person we need as a forest agent. Defeating Lukos doesn't mean we've sorted out all the worlds' problems. Still plenty of need for new apprentices."

Jem's green eyes were sparkling. "They've agreed to take me on, too!" he said. "They do train some agents who don't have magic. Usually they work in pairs, with an agent who does. So…" He looked at her expectantly.

Dora raised one eyebrow at him.

"Come on, Dora," he wheedled. "We're a team. Aren't we?"

She could feel the corner of her mouth twitching upwards. "OK. I suppose I'd better stick with you. Who knows what mayhem you'll cause across the worlds if you're on your own…"

Jem whooped and blew her a kiss. "I knew you'd agree!" he said. "We'll be the best forest agents they've ever had!"

"What about Roland Castle, though?" said Dora to the Druid. "Won't you need a new apprentice?"

The Druid grinned. "I'm not going back to Roland Castle," he said. "I'm planning to try my luck in Wemworthy for a while. I thought I might see if they'd give me a job back at my old place."

"Designing computer games?" said Simon, sitting up. "Really?"

"Yes," said the Druid. "I've got this idea for a

multiple worlds adventure. You have to find four bits of amber, save the worlds… I think it will be a hit."

"So, will you be living with us?" said Cat, with a glance at her mother. Florence coloured.

"Er, no," said the Druid, with a cough. "I'll get a place… umm… round the corner. But I expect I'll be over quite a bit. To – er – see you all. And Mother, of course."

"Oh, I shan't be there," said Great-Aunt Irene with a smile. She had been flitting around the clearing, her outline getting fainter, more silvery, less defined – but now she returned to stand next to the Druid, and patted him on the head with one silvery hand. "I think you'll all do just fine without me, you know. And I really shouldn't be here any more. The amber passed on, and now it's beyond all of us. Time for me to go, I believe."

"Oh no, you can't!" cried Simon. "We'll… we'll really miss you!"

"I know, dear boy," said Great-Aunt Irene, floating over and touching him on the cheek with one ghostly finger. "And you, too, Cat!" She tilted Cat's chin up with one hand, and wiped a tear away with the other. "I'm glad I could be part of it all with you, but really, I'm tired now. It's time to go."

She returned to the Druid, and stood solemnly in front of him. "Goodbye, Louis. Look after them all."

"Goodbye, Mother," he said, standing up. He rested his warm brown hands on her silvery shoulders for a moment, then bent and kissed her on the forehead.

Dora swallowed, and found her vision blurred with tears as the silvery outline gradually faded. Just as the ghostly figure was disappearing, Queen Igraine rushed into the clearing.

"Have I missed her?" she gasped. "Has she left already?"

Great-Aunt Irene lifted her hand and waved faintly. Igraine waved back, and then dabbed her eyes with her lace shawl as the last bits of silvery dust twinkled and were gone.

The misty portal hung in the clearing, shimmering. Albert stood next to it, twirling the key to his lock-up round one finger.

"So," he said. "Who's for Wemworthy?"

The Druid held out one hand to Florence and

the other to Cat. "Proper baths," he said dreamily. "Wifi. Motorbikes. Flushing toilets." He smiled crookedly at Dora. "I'll be back," he said. "To check up on you and Jem."

She nodded and brushed a tear away with one sleeve. The Druid strode across the clearing and enveloped her in a huge bear hug. "You'll be fine, Dora," he whispered. "I'll see you soon. I promise."

"Darien?" said Albert, gesturing to the young pirate. "I've got a token back in my lock-up that'll get you to Belhaven. The Sea's still touching the port, so you should be able to get a ship to Rode, find the *Mermaid*."

Darien nodded and stepped forward eagerly. "And maybe," he said, with a slight bow to Cat, "I could come back, after I'm settled, and you could take me somewhere on that 'date' you mentioned."

Cat laughed. "Yes, of course. I'd love to!"

Florence gave Darien a rather stern look. "No wine," she said. "And back by half past nine at the latest."

He bowed. "Of course. Whatever you say," he agreed, and Florence gave him an approving smile.

Albert turned to Inanna. "You'll be headin'

back to Ur-Akkad, then, young lady?"

She nodded, her dark braids rustling. "I need to find out what happened. I need to see if I can help restore some… order."

"You'll do a good job, my dear, I'm sure," said Queen Igraine warmly. "And I believe you are taking someone along to help?"

Inanna blushed and glanced at Sir Bedwyr standing beside her. He twirled his sword happily.

"I am Princess Inanna's sworn knight," he said, with a bow. "Where she leads, I will follow!"

Jem nudged Dora, and grinned. "He'll be *much* better at that than I would have been," he whispered. "She's far too bossy for me…"

Dora nodded and tried to suppress a laugh at the thought of Jem being ordered around for the rest of his life by Inanna. "I think being a forest agent will suit you much better than being a knight, Jem. Knights have to be chivalrous and honourable, and play by the rules. I can't think of a single rule at Roland Castle you hadn't broken at least twice by the time you were *ten*."

Jem looked a little sheepish, but his eyes were "Jem Tollpuddle, Forest Agent," he said. od ring to it, hasn't it?"

"It has indeed," said the Druid. He clapped Jem on the back, and then strode to the portal. "Just make sure you work hard, Jem, and do what Dora tells you. Or you might end up an ex-agent before you finish your apprenticeship!"

"OK," said Albert. "Time to go."

"Simon?' said Florence.

Simon was standing by the portal with a mutinous expression on his face.

"I'm not going," he said.

"What?" said Florence sharply.

"I'm not going," repeated Simon obstinately. "Unless you promise that we can come back in the holidays. I want to learn to use magic. I want to learn to use a sword. And *I* want to be a forest agent as well!"

There was a moment's silence as Florence frowned at him and the Druid looked apprehensive. Then she gave a rueful smile.

"Of course you can come back, Simon," she said. "It's what your dad would have wanted. It's what Lou tried to tell me all along. And it's probably something I should have agreed to a long time ago. We'll all come back – often. But you still have to go to school and give yourself a chance in our world as well. So you can choose, when it comes to it."

Simon whooped, and gave his mum a hug. He raised his hand to Dora and Jem.

"I'll be joining you," he said. "No question. Live in my world, when I can use magic and work for the Great Forest? You must be joking!"

Cat grinned at them. "Me too!" she said. "You'll be seeing a lot of us, don't worry."

One by one, they waved, and smiled, and walked into the mist of the portal – the Druid, Florence, Darien, Cat, Albert and finally, with a wink and a thumbs up, Simon. The portal disappeared with a faint pop.

"Right," said Jem. "Who's for some more food? I'm *starving*!"

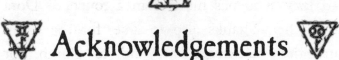

Acknowledgements

I'd like to express my thanks to a number of people who've had a hand not just in this book but in the previous two as well. Emma Goldhawk is a fabulous editor who helped shape the whole series and did a great job on the first two books. Thanks are also due to the excellent Matilda Johnson, who took over on the second book and shepherded the final volume through a rather daunting set of deadlines with skill and encouragement. David Wyatt's covers have enhanced all three books, as well as my previous ones, and I'm very grateful to him for the collaboration.

Stories inevitably draw for inspiration on real people and events. Thanks to my sister, Celi, for accompanying me on numerous fantasy adventures when we were children. To my dad, a mix of the Druid and Albert Jemmet, who continues to battle the dark-suited men of the National Radiological Protection Board. To my brother Joe, whose eBay sword really did cut Mum's washing to pieces and destroy her sofa. To Izzy, who has more than a touch of Dora about her. Thanks also to Zoe, for the Latin and the encouragement, and to Philip, for endless thoughtful rereading. And to Max, for being Max.

Finally, my thanks to Laura Cecil, to whom this book is dedicated, for her advice, humour and insight, for always being at the end of a phone, and for knowing just what needs changing.

ABOUT THE AUTHOR

C. J. Busby grew up living on boats with her family and spent most of her childhood with her nose in a book – even when walking along the road. Luckily she survived to grow up, but she still carried on reading whenever she could. After studying social anthropology at university, she lived in a South Indian fishing village and did research for her PhD. She currently lives in Devon with her three children, and borrows their books whenever they let her.

To find out more, please visit:
www.cjbusby.co.uk